WITHIN THE FLAMES

SEVEN WARDENS BOOK 4

LAURA GREENWOOD

SKYE MACKINNON

Peryton Press

CONTENTS

To anyone who's ever had a WTF moment. Or is about to by reading this book.

BEFORE YOU START

The Seven Wardens series is a reverse harem, one woman and multiple love interests. Macey does not have to choose.

Please note that the authors of this book are from the UK, and as such, spellings and some turns of phrase will appear in British English.

You can find a glossary at the end of this book.

Due to an absence of waffles, Macey's magic became a little violent (okay, maybe there were other reasons for that, but let's focus on the waffles). To help, Ronan offered to sleep with her - and ended up being part of her harem. Now she has four guys: one incubus, two wraiths and a selkie who can't shift. Yay Macey!

However, they don't have time for much sexiness (nor for waffles), because trouble is brewing on the horizon: the Great Orca is terrorising the selkies, while in Belgium, something is happening to the Earth magic. The Wardens decide to split up, and while Jared and Macey go on a little trip to meet the Kabouters and Kludde, the others fight the Orca. They wouldn't have succeeded though, but Macey returned just in time to do some awesome magic and rescue them all. As a reward, she got two chapters worth of sex. Lucky girl.

They decide it's finally time to face the Mahoun/Voice, so they gather their allies. Sadly, only the Kabouters, kelpies and a few na fir ghorma listened to their call. Worst of all, while visiting the seelie, Flint was injured and is now without any fire magic.

Can they save him before it's too late?

Will they finally, finally get their waffles?

THE SEVEN WARDENS

Water: Macey (Kelpie)
Wind: Cam (Wraith)
Fire: Flint (Wraith)
Earth: Jared (Incubus)
Ice: Izban (Mage)
Lightning: Amber (Beithir)
Air: Talia (Seelie hosted within Macey)

ONE

Macey paced back and forth outside the bedroom, wanting answers but so far having received none. The kelpie physician had been in with Flint for over an hour and she was starting to worry.

"He'll be alright," Jared assured her, rubbing his hand up and down her back.

"Sure," she muttered. She was even more worried than she was trying to let on. Flint's magic was gone. Which, on the surface, wasn't that big of a deal, but it definitely was. It didn't just mean that one of them had less of an ability to defend themselves, but it would mean the Warden magic itself wouldn't be at full strength.

What worried her most was the lack of similar powers to Flint's fire. If her or Izban were out of action, they could do their best to cover for each other. Same with the Air Warden inside of her; she could be replaced by Cam's wind magic. It'd be more difficult for Amber's lightning or Jared's earth, but Macey was sure both would be easier to compensate for than actual flames.

The door creaked and one of the kelpies emerged, a grim look on his face. "I don't think there's anything we can do, Your Highness." He nodded his head in reverence, making Macey scowl. What was the point of her having a stupid title if it didn't help her get things done?

"Thank you," she acknowledged. Even if they hadn't done quite what she wanted him to do.

"If you forgive me for being so bold, Your Highness, I believe you won't find anyone who can help you here. Fire beings are rare, and there are none I've heard of in these isles."

"Do you have any idea where I will find some?" She crossed her fingers behind her back, hoping he'd have at least some idea of what she should do.

Indecision crossed the physician's face. "I'm not sure, but while I was a young kelpie, I travelled Europe. I heard tales of lampads while I was in Greece. I'm not even sure if the nymphs are real, but legend says they used torches to accompany the goddess, Hecate, on her travels."

"The gods aren't real," Macey pointed out.

"Maybe not. But I'm sure you're aware there's some truth in every legend by now, Princess."

"That is true," she admitted, thinking over the various people assembled here and what she'd thought of them before they'd actually met.

"You might need to do some research first. Though the legend is Greek, I doubt that's where they are now."

"Thank you, Jerome. Your insights have been invaluable."

"You're welcome. I hope to see your husband back in full powers soon." He dipped his head and left the room.

"Husband?" Jared raised his eyebrows.

"Yes. According to the kelpies, you're all my husbands."

"A little greedy, don't you think?"

"You're the ones who encouraged me to be with you all," she countered.

"You didn't have to go with it," he murmured, leaning forward so their lips nearly touched. "But I'm glad you did. The sexual energy you let off could keep me sated for years."

"I hope it doesn't," she teased.

Jared laughed softly, not breaking the intimacy of the moment. "I'm starting to think you're insatiable, little kelpie."

"Only when it comes to the four of you."

"Unless you go and add another one to your collection." He smirked, a glint in his eyes that had her questioning just how serious he was. Maybe he did want that after all.

"I think four is enough for me."

"You said that about three."

"And I meant it." But she couldn't feel bad when four had brought her Rónàn. Her selkie was just another compliment to their group, even if he wasn't a Warden.

"Are you going to kiss me?"

Instead of answering, Jared pressed his lips against hers and kissed her chastely. It'd be a disappointment if she wasn't aware of Flint lying in the next room.

"Go to him," Jared said once they'd broken apart. "I know you need to."

"Thank you." She kissed him quickly, before tearing herself away and retreating to the room Malan had assigned them.

"Hey," he croaked at her.

"Hey," she whispered. "How are you feeling?" She stood completely still, unable to move either way into the room. It was just too painful seeing him lie there without any way of helping.

"Empty."

Macey swallowed the guilt she was feeling. She'd sent him off to deal with the Seelie and this was what had happened. She wished she'd been able to do more, but hopefully she could rectify that.

"I'm going to try and make things right," she told him.

"I know," he replied.

"How much time do you have?"

A thoughtful look crossed over his face. "I don't know. I've never been without my magic before, but as far as I'm aware, I don't need it to live."

"But?"

"But nothing," he defended.

"No, not but nothing. I could hear it in your voice." She crossed her arms under her chest and gave him what she hoped was a stern look.

"But nothing."

"Flint." She gave him a stern look, and he sighed.

"I'm pretty sure I'm human right now."

"As in..."

"I don't have any magic, so I'm a little bit more...vulnerable."

She gave him a blank stare, not quite knowing what he was getting at.

"I could die, Macey. Pretty easily as far as I can tell. Some of the things we've been through together, I wouldn't be able to survive at all."

"Fuck."

"My thoughts exactly," he joked.

"What can I do?" she whispered, closing the gap between herself and the bed, taking his hand in hers.

"What was your plan?"

"The lampads."

Flint gave the statement some consideration. "That might actually work. If you can bring one of their flames back, I can use it to try and kickstart my powers."

"You can't come with me?"

He shook his head. "No, I won't be able to. I'm human. If I look into their light...well, it's not worth thinking about. But also, to get to them, you'll probably have to pass some kind of test, and you won't be allowed to take anyone else with you. If you have help, you fail automatically."

Macey swallowed the lump that was resting in her throat. Her task had just become a lot more difficult.

And it wasn't helped by having a horde of allies waiting outside, ready to be sent into battle. She couldn't really tell them all to go home, but she also couldn't start the fight against the Mahoun without Flint's powers. She instinctively knew that they were going to need all seven Wardens to be able to succeed.

"I should talk to Malan, maybe he knows where I can find a lampad."

"According to the legends, they're in the Underworld, but let's hope that's just a myth," Flint said weakly.

Macey grimaced. "Yes, let's hope so. I don't have the time to walk through Hell like Dante."

She gave Flint a kiss and headed back into the living room where her other men were waiting together with a whole lot of other people. Representatives of the various allies, she assumed. Malan was hovering in one corner, talking to an old kabouter whose beard was touching the floor. She walked towards them, nodding and smiling at the kelpies and na fir ghorma who were all crowded into the small room. She doubted Malan had ever had this many guests before.

She cleared her throat when she'd reached the prophet. He turned and grinned at her.

"I assume you're wanting to save your man?"

"Ehm, yes." She looked at the kabouter who hastily left. "What do you know about lampads?"

"Oh, the daughters of Nyx, good thinking."

"Nyx?"

"The Goddess of the Night. She brings the darkness, so her daughters carry torches to help travellers reach their mother. I met one once, a long time ago. She was excellent at bringing an extinguished torch back to life."

He winked and Macey cringed. He didn't mean what she thought he did, right? That was disgusting.

"Where did you meet her?" she asked quickly.

"At a bar in London. We went to a Shakespeare play later... She was quite taken by young Will."

"Wait, you met Shakespeare?"

He chuckled. "I'm older than I look. Now let me see if I can give you a confusing and mysterious prophecy."

She stared at him. Did he really just say that?

"How about direct and helpful advice?" she asked, and he laughed again.

"Maybe I'm feeling nice today... or maybe I just want to get rid of all these people beleaguering my house." He closed his eyes for a moment and when he opened them again, his pupils were enlarged and glowing around the edges. "You don't have to go to Greece. There's a lampad couple who might be able to help. I can't see where exactly they are. Some-where underground, but it's not natural. It's a building that's underground. And it's in a city."

Macey waited for him to continue, but he didn't say anything more.

"So that's you being direct?" she asked in exasper-ation. "How is that supposed to help? There are thousands of cities on this planet, and I bet most of them have some kind of underground buildings. I can't very well search every parking garage in the world."

Malan smiled patiently. "No, you couldn't. You're

very lucky you have an extremely talented prophet at your disposal."

Macey couldn't help but roll her eyes. Talented, maybe, but not very forthcoming with information. She stayed quiet though, letting him do his prophet thing. His eyes were still glowing slightly.

"The city has towers..."

This time, Macey sighed. Of course it did, just like every second bleeding city.

"By the watery waves, could you please just give me some directions?"

Malan frowned. "Patience, young kelpie. Oh, I can see waffles in your future... no, let's not get distracted. As I said, towers. No, one tower. The Tower. Of London. And it's not a building that's underground."

"It's the tube," Macey helpfully supplied. "The underground railway. You do know that the tube network is massive? Do those lampads ride the trains all day? Or what are they doing down there?"

Malan grinned. "That's for you to find out. Just follow your nose."

"Really? That's it?" Macey was getting annoyed. She hoped her hair wasn't changing colour. There were other kelpies in the room and it would be bad form to show how she didn't have her temper under control. She was their Princess, after all.

"Yes, now go while I try and entertain all these

masses." He looked around with a smirk. "Bring some food with you on the way back. Everyone will be hungry by then."

"Is that a prophecy?"

"It's common sense," Malan muttered. "Off with you, and remember, don't let any of your men help if the lampads give you a task to prove your worthiness. It might disqualify you."

Macey sighed and returned to her men, who had assembled around Flint's bedside.

"I'm going to London," she announced and they all stared at her.

"London? Why?" Jared finally asked.

"According to Malan, there are lampads living there. Somewhere underground."

"London is big," Cam said with a frown. "I assume he was mysterious and vague as always?"

Macey nodded. "Yes, but at least we now know the city. That's more than what he said before. And surely it can't be that difficult to find someone in London."

Jared snickered. "You've never been there, have you?"

She cringed. "No, but I've seen it on television. It's big, but the underground system is quite organised, right? There are maps and guides."

"Yes, and thousands of people," Flint muttered

weakly. "You'll never find someone in those crowds. Did Malan say anything else?"

Macey shrugged. "Follow your nose, that's all he said. Do lampads have a certain smell?"

"Smoke?" Cam suggested. "Or maybe... I don't know. But usually, Malan's words end up making sense at some point, even if they didn't before. Hopefully, that's what's going to happen once you get to London."

TWO

She jumped back as the bus hurtled past, scowling at the traffic. She'd not liked the thought of London before, but now she was here she liked it even less.

"Which way now?" Rónàn asked.

"How should I know?" she snapped, instantly regretting being so short with him. It wasn't his fault none of them knew what they were doing.

"What did Malan say again?" Jared placed a soothing hand on the small of her back as he spoke, offering her the comfort she needed.

"He described the Tower of London, but I doubt it's that easy."

"Why not?" Rónàn asked.

"Because it's Malan," Jared muttered. "He doesn't do straight forward."

"Maybe this time he is? I've not heard of him before, but he seems to actually care about the fate of the world."

"Don't be fooled," Macey mumbled under her breath. She'd had enough experience with Malan to know he wouldn't care for anyone but himself and his food. Slightly odd interests for a dead prophet, but there was no denying either of them.

"It's worth a try," Cam pointed out.

Macey nodded. While she hated admitting it was their best lead, it was. And that didn't mean much to her.

"Which way do we need to go?" she asked her incubus. Bringing him had been imperative for going underground. Hopefully he'd actually be able to sense things through all this noise.

"This way, I think." He peered over the top of the map he was holding, an uneasy look on his face.

Macey wasn't convinced, but said nothing. She was just glad they were finally getting somewhere.

The four of them dodged through the streets, only just avoiding the people who seemed to be everywhere. She coughed, the dirty air tickling her nose and threatening to make her sneeze. This wasn't the thing she'd had in mind when lampads had been mentioned.

"Are we nearly there?" She crossed her fingers, hoping one of them would say yes.

"We just need to cross that bridge and we'll be there," Jared muttered, not taking his eyes off his map long enough to actually be able to tell if they were going the right way or not.

Macey made a mental note not to let Jared map read again. Certainly not if they were in a city. Though why they'd go back to one as big as this was a little beyond her.

Heat clung all around them, making the air heavy and difficult to breath. She definitely wasn't leaving the country again. She'd go back to Scotland and stay there for good. Or even better, go back to her men's house. There wasn't any pollution there and the house would cater to their every need. It would be cool all year round.

"Macey!" Rónàn cried, tugging the back of her shirt and dragging her back onto the path.

She scowled at the road. Cars weren't anywhere near this bad where she came from. They certainly didn't nearly try and kill her every thirty seconds.

"Get us underground," she begged.

"Just around this corner," Jared said, turning towards a set of stairs at the edge of the bridge.

He walked as if in a trance, taking them closer and closer to the river.

Macey turned up her nose. The stench coming from it was enough to turn her stomach. She loved water, but she'd be staying as away from this as she could. No one would even be able to pay her to dip her toe in.

"Are you sure we're going the right way?"

Jared didn't reply, heading under the bridge and into the darkness. Instead of coming out the other side, as Macey had expected, they turned to the right and through a hole in the wall she hadn't even seen.

Nerves fluttered around her stomach. Common sense said not to go down into the dark. Nothing good would be there, but she knew she had to go underground so she could help Flint.

Dripping sounded all around her, the wet splashes of droplets hitting uneven stone floors lending the tunnel an eerie atmosphere. Macey found herself wondering what could be lurking down here. In her experience, there was always something waiting and it was hardly ever good. This would be a perfect place for the Mahoun or one of his kind to lie in wait.

Then again, it wouldn't be that easy to find him, or else they could have dealt with him already.

Their footsteps echoed around the room, the only sounds apart from the dripping water. Macey shivered. She didn't like this one bit.

"Are you sure this is the way to the lampads?" she whispered, not wanting to risk speaking any louder.

"Malan said to follow our noses," Jared pointed out.

"Are you?" she asked quickly.

Jared threw her a disapproving look and she lowered her head, feeling bad about doubting him.

"This place doesn't make me want to shift," Rónàn muttered.

"Me neither," she replied, thinking of the river above. Normally she'd love splashing about in any kind of water. Not so much here.

"It's not exactly great for me either," Cam added, slipping an arm around Macey and pulling her to him.

They walked in silence for a couple of yards, each lost in their own thoughts and concerns.

"Do you think Flint's okay?" Her voice shook as she spoke, but she didn't care. They all knew how she felt about him, she didn't need to hide it.

"I haven't had any messages from him," Cam said evenly.

"Does that work still?"

"I honestly don't know," Cam admitted. "I'm thinking maybe not. But it was his fire that was taken, not the rest of him."

Macey frowned, not sure she quite agreed with Cam's assessment. Her magic and shifting were all tied up in one neat little package, it seemed unlikely that Flint's was any different. It was probably best if she didn't say what she was thinking though, she didn't want to freak any of them out more than she had to.

They continued on through the strange tunnel,

their eyes slowly getting used to the darkness, but not enough to see the uneven ground. Macey kept stumbling over rocks and so did the men. The ground was getting wetter and their feet were making squelching sounds that echoed through the tunnel.

They stayed quiet, all of them aware that they were in unfamiliar territory. Who knew what lived down there. Rats, certainly, but if there were lampads, then maybe some other mythical beings had made this their home as well. And those usually meant trouble.

"Wait, I hear something," Rónàn suddenly whispered. Macey stopped, but she couldn't hear anything besides the dripping of water and the heaviness of their breaths. On the other hand, her kelpie ears were good underwater, but on earth, they were just as good as those of humans.

"Whispers," Cam confirmed. "Far ahead. Let's be careful."

They continued, even slower than before. Macey still couldn't hear any voices, but Rónàn and Cam were obviously following their direction. Maybe there were some homeless people sleeping rough in these tunnels.

Flint's fire would have come in handy to give them some light, but of course, his absence was why they were here. She hoped he was alright. Seeing him so powerless had hurt something deep within her. She was going to make someone pay for it, whether it was the sidhe, the Mahoun or someone else. No one messed with her men.

Finally, after what felt like several minutes of stumbling through the dark, she heard the whispers. She stopped to listen, to try and understand what the voices were saying, but it didn't seem to be English.

"Can you hear them now?" Cam whispered and she nodded, before realising he probably couldn't see her.

"Yes," she whispered back. "Do you understand what they're saying?"

"No idea. I thought it would get clearer once we got closer, but whatever language they're speaking isn't one I'm familiar with."

Well, that excluded at least four or five languages. Cam talked in his sleep, and not always in a language Macey could understand. She only knew English and some Gaelic that Aunt Nessie had taught her, but both wraiths had travelled the world and were a lot better educated than Macey was. The Loch school only got you so far and there was no kelpie university. Her father hadn't allowed her to go to Ben Vair, the school for supernaturals that Amber had attended, which meant her education had been very much focussed on living underwater.

"What do we do now?" Jared asked, sniffing the air. "Do we surprise them? If it's the lampads, only

Macey should talk to them, but I'm not sure I want her to go there on her own until we know what we're dealing with."

"Agreed," Rónàn grumbled, protectively putting a hand on Macey's shoulder. "After what happened to Flint, we stick together."

She could live with that. The more, the merrier, especially in dangerous situations like this one. Not that she actually knew if it was going to be danger-ous, but in the past few weeks, she'd learned that life was a lot more dangerous than she'd ever imagined. Side effect of being one of the Wardens.

"Let's go then," she said, walking past the men and towards the voices. "It sounds like there's only two or three of them, so we should be able to deal with them, if they're hostile."

The guys followed her. Cam seemed tempted to take the lead again, but Macey didn't let him. She might have to deal with the lampads on her own anyway.

A flickering light suddenly appeared in the distance. A fire? A torch?

"Hello?" someone shouted, his voice echoing through the tunnel, reverberating all around Macey. He sounded old.

"Hello!" she called back. "Can we come closer?"

Laughter greeted her words. "I don't bite, unless you've brought food."

Macey turned to look at her men, but even with the tiny bit of light, she was unable to see their expressions. She shrugged and continued towards the light. The whispers she'd heard before had stopped now. Was the old man one of them? Had he been whispering in another language?

This was all very strange. The sooner they got out of these tunnels and back into daylight - non-London daylight, preferably - the better.

When they got closer, the light turned out to be a campfire, built with large slabs of wood onto the concrete floor. The man, whoever he was, had chosen one of the few dry spots in these catacombs. Where did he get the wood though?

A silhouette was barely visible behind the shine of the fire. A large man, but it wasn't obvious whether he was human or not. He could have been anything, really.

"Who are you?" Macey asked when they were close enough to talk without shouting.

"You come into my home and ask me that?"

Jared coughed. "His home? I can imagine nicer places."

"Don't you dare belittle my house," the man snarled, suddenly sounding a lot less friendly. "You of all people should know better, incubus."

He spat out the final word. Okay, he was someone who didn't like incubi. Not that it was something unusual; most people were scared of them.

"Me of all people?" Jared asked, taken aback. "Why... ooooh."

"What is it?" Macey whispered.

"An illusion," Jared said slowly. "It's all an illusion."

"I never thought they'd pick children as the final Wardens," the man muttered dismissively. "You don't seem ready yet. Can't even spot an illusion."

"Children?" Cam seemed offended. "I'm likely older than you are."

The man laughed. "I doubt that very much. But come, we have much to discuss. Please be aware that this is a sanctuary, and as such, everyone is welcome here, no matter the species. Any attacks on residents will be punished severely."

Macey's eyes widened at his words. "We're not here to hurt anyone," she reassured him. "We just need to find someone."

"I know."

Somehow, the man reminded her of Malan. Cryptic, impolite, arrogant. Maybe he was Malan's lost twin? Who wasn't a ghost yet?

He'd already turned around and was walking away from the fire. She still hadn't seen his face, but when she'd passed the fire, she could at least see his back. He had wings. Black, leathery wings.

"What is he?" she whispered to her men. "Some kind of demon?"

"He's a daimon," Cam gasped, stopping in his tracks. "I didn't think they still existed."

"A demon?"

He shook his head. "A daimon. Big difference. They're guides, advisors. Some say they're spirits sent from the afterlife to guide mortals. Others say they're an ancient race of beings with unimaginable powers. Point is, they're rare, powerful and we really don't want to anger him."

"He doesn't like me," Jared complained quietly. "I seem to be angering him simply by being here."

Macey reached out to the incubus, taking his hand. "He'll just have to deal with it. We're here as a team, and whether this is his home or not, we stay together."

She didn't feel as confident as her words made her sound, but the men didn't need to know that.

"Hurry!" the daimon shouted from far ahead. He'd almost merged with the shadows in the distance, the light of the fire no longer reaching him. Macey sighed softly and began to walk as fast as she dared, hoping that there weren't any rocks to stumble over.

"What is a daimon doing in London?" Cam was muttering behind her, but she ignored him. They weren't going to find out by speculating.

The tunnel slowly began to widen until they reached the entrance to a large cavern.

"Wait!" Jared suddenly shouted just when Macey was about to walk through the stone archway.

She stopped in her tracks, turning around to look at him.

"It's an illusion!" He pressed past her and held out his hands towards the cavern. "Now that I know what to look for, I can feel it. Something is behind there and it's not just an empty cave."

"Well, it would make sense," Macey mused. "He called it his home, after all, and I doubt it's that fire pit from earlier."

"We should proceed with caution," Rónàn said, speaking for the first time in a while. He'd been staying in the background while they'd been talking to the daimon, and even now, he was keeping back. Was he afraid? Uncomfortable in the dark, perhaps?

"Let me go first." Jared carefully took a step forward, his arms still outstretched. "Wow, it's warm," he said after two more steps. "Positively hot."

"Lampads?" Macey asked hopefully.

Jared took a deep breath and stepped through the archway - and disappeared. All Macey saw was the same dark cavern as she had before, but Jared had clearly walked into something else. The illusion was strong, even though she knew it wasn't real, she couldn't see anything besides the cave.

"Jared!" she shouted, ready to run after him.

A muffled cough came from in front of her. "It's fine, come on through. It tickles."

Rónàn stepped closer to Macey and took her hand. "Let's do this."

Illustration: Daimon

THREE

Together, they walked through the archway. Jared had been right, it tickled, like a thousand feathers were gently drawn over Macey's skin. She let go of Rónàn's hand and ran her fingers over her arms to get rid of whatever was tickling her, but there was nothing there.

Everything was black until suddenly - colour erupted all around them.

"What the fucking waves," Macey muttered as she took in the landscape around her. They'd stumbled into a party, a massive, loud party full of light strobes and burning fires. The noise was unbelievable and she was tempted to put her hands over her ears.

They were still in a cave, so huge that she couldn't see the ceiling, but instead of being empty as it seemed before, there were houses everywhere, dotted around the place like a child had played with its lego set and then kicked the pieces in random directions. Some of the houses looked like they were clearly not following the rules of gravity, with balconies larger than the actual house, and walls that were bending outwards. Fires were burning in iron baskets all over the place and lampoons were hanging from ropes spanned between buildings.

And then there were the people. Hundreds of them, dancing in the streets, clapping, stamping on the ground, jumping.

"I didn't expect this," Jared said dryly. He was waiting for them, his beautiful features illuminated by the fire. Was it his incubus or Macey's hormones that made her want to rip off his clothes?

She forced herself to look away from him. Some of the partygoers must have been having similar thoughts: they were in various stages of undress, with couples half-hidden in alleyways and others doing it openly in front of everybody else.

This was as hedonistic as anything Macey had ever seen.

"Now I know why he doesn't want incubi here," Jared chuckled, pointing at a couple who were busy plunging their tongues into each other's mouths. "I could feast off this for months."

His eyes were glowing slightly and a sharp tug

went through Macey's lower belly. She really wanted to be close to him, to touch him, to kiss him, to...

Suddenly, Rónàn stepped past her and pressed his lips against Jared's. He wrapped his thick arms around the incubus and pulled him close, shielding him from view.

"What the..." Macey was speechless. Rónàn? And Jared? Kissing?

"Tune it down, Jared!" Cam shouted. "Even I want to jump your bones just now."

Jared pushed Rónàn away from him, struggling against the selkie who was clearly stronger than the incubus.

"I'm trying," Jared muttered, his teeth clenched and the little muscle in his forehead bulging.

Something warred within Macey, trying to counteract the lust she was feeling towards him. But then, why should she? He was hers, she could be with him, all it would take was...

"Jared! NOW!" Cam yelled, sounding angrier than Macey had ever heard him. It cut through her haze slightly, though she could still feel the urge to get to Jared. It wasn't letting up any time soon.

Rónàn struggled against Jared, trying to kiss him again. Jealousy welled up within her and the ends of her hair began to turn green. Jared was *hers*. No one else would touch him.

The lust vanquished for a moment, she stepped

forward and between the two men, grabbing each by their shirt and pushing them away from one another. Her nails sharpened and turned into claws, ripping the fabric.

"Hands off," she said sternly. She felt her nostrils flaring and her eyes hardening.

Without being fully aware of what she was doing, she threw Rónàn towards the wall. His back slammed against it and a grunt escaped him, but Macey was too gone to care. Lust and wrath coiled up inside her, controlling her every move.

She could hear the murmur of voices letting her know her men were still trying to get through to her, but she didn't pay them any heed. Macey stalked towards her selkie, determined to make him pay for what he'd done.

A booming laugh sounded, cutting through the rage.

"Well, well, that wasn't what I expected."

Macey turned to the source of the voice, looking the daimon up and down. He was certainly an attractive looking man, other than the wings. Though something about them was magnificent and powerful. Maybe it was their size. They could rival a normal man's height.

"Who are you?" she asked, her voice raspy through the anger.

"Lucian, but you can call me Luc," he replied, his

smirk growing all the wider. "Would you like some help controlling your incubus?"

Macey nodded. She didn't like the idea of restraining Jared in any way, but given the circumstances, she needed to do something.

Luc waved his hand and glittering grey cuffs appeared around Jared's wrists. He sighed in the same relief that Macey was now feeling too.

The anger receded along with the lust, and horror set in as she realised what she'd done. Spinning on her heels, she rushed towards Rónàn, who was slumped on the floor, rubbing his head.

"I'm so sorry, please forgive me?" she begged, falling to her knees beside him.

"What happened?" His brow creased as he tried to work it out.

Macey threw a confused look at Cam, hoping he'd be able to help her out. He shook his head, clearly as perplexed by the situation as she was.

"I threw you against a wall," she admitted quietly.

"That's why it hurts then."

She nodded. "I'm sorry. You kissed Jared and I got angry and..."

"I kissed Jared?" The confusion on Rónàn's face deepened even more.

"Yes, yes, you kissed the incubus, the kelpie got angry and the wraith just yelled. What a lovely little family," Luc said jovially.

"We have names you know," Macey snapped, this anger having nothing to do with jealousy and everything to do with disrespect. She was the kelpie princess, how dare this daimon she didn't even know treat her this way.

"I'm well aware. And titles too. I believe four of you are Wardens, though where you left the other three is beyond me."

"They're safe," Macey assured him, thinking of Amber and Izban back at Malan's house. They'd be sorting their army out if everything was going to plan. And keeping Flint safe.

"I doubt that. You wouldn't be here if they were."

"You sound awfully amused to be talking about such dire circumstances," Macey retorted, getting to her feet and offering her hand to Rónàn. He took it, and she helped him to his feet.

"Why wouldn't I be amused? Last I checked, the world was still in a shambles thanks to you."

Macey's eyes bore into him, the anger rising inside her again. If Luc wasn't careful, she'd throw every bit of water magic she had at him and more. Maybe she'd even be able to call on Air to help her with the attack.

"You're not going to want to do that. Not if you want my help," Luc said.

"How do you know what I'm thinking?" she demanded.

"You're not very good at hiding what you're thinking, it's written all over your face."

Luc turned away from them all, his wings batting against his back as he stood and gazed out at the writhing mass of people below them.

"What is this place?" Macey stepped forward to stand beside him, taking in the sight herself.

Without Jared's magic influencing her, there wasn't anything remotely sexy about the mass below. It was just too many limbs and mouths, all hungry and desperate for flesh. She might enjoy sex, but she wanted it to mean something too. It had to be with her men.

"A pit of sin," Luc answered.

"That doesn't tell me a lot."

"It's a test, Macey. Everything down here is a test."

He blood ran cold as she considered the implications of that. "But..."

"Not that kind of test."

"How do you know all this?" she asked in wonder.

"Let's just say we have a mutual friend."

"Malan," she muttered darkly.

Luc laughed. "Yes, him. Infuriating, isn't he?"

"That's one word for him," Cam muttered darkly from behind.

Macey ignored him and glanced at Jared who was looking at his cuffs with a curious expression on his face. She'd have to ask him about that when Luc had finished being as cryptic and infuriating as Malan himself.

"That still doesn't explain anything," she pointed out.

"Tell me, Macey, did you really expect seeing the lampads to be as easy as just turning up at their door?"

She sighed. "I'd hoped."

"That's a no, then."

"Let's just say past experience suggested it wouldn't be that easy."

"I thought as much. Incubus, I'd stop staring at those cuffs, you'll give yourself a headache," Luc said without even looking in Jared's direction. "Just trust me that you'll need them to keep blocking your powers."

"I can't say I care for it," Jared muttered.

"It's preferable," Rónàn responded.

Macey snorted. "Alright you two, stop it. If Lucien says it's necessary, then we need to take his word for it."

"And how do we know he's to be trusted?" Jared snarled. "Maybe he's blocking my powers for an entirely different reason."

His words echoed around Macey's head as they registered and she wondered if there wasn't some truth in them.

Lucien's head fell back and he let out a hearty laugh. "I guess you won't know unless you try and trust me," he teased.

Macey frowned, not sure what to make of it at all. Could she trust a daimon? She longed to ask Cam, but given the proximity of them all, there was no way she could do that without Luc becoming aware of it and her diplomatic training wouldn't allow her to insult anyone quite like that.

"I will trust you," she told him. "But I'm also wary. I'm not idiotic enough to let my guard down."

"Smart," Luc answered. "You can never be too careful in this day and age."

"You still haven't explained what this test is."

"You tell me, Princess. It's your mind that's conjured it."

"I doubt that," she countered.

"Actually, I wouldn't," Cam interrupted.

"What do you mean?"

"I've heard talk of the lampads before, they're an odd race and their magic can span far and wide. It's possible that their tests have extended this far and are already in the process of working out how best to test you."

"What the wraith said," Luc added.

"He has a name," Macey ground out, unhappy with the daimon's lack of respect for the people around him.

"Yes, yes, he's called Camdan, I'm aware of you all, Macey, Jared and Rónàn. I know your pasts and your secrets. Make no mistake of it."

"How do you know all this?"

"How does a butterfly flap its wings? There are some things we may never know."

"I think that's a lie."

She stepped forward so there was barely space between them. She could feel Luc's breath on her cheek and the warmth radiating from his body. Rather than being repulsed, she found herself reassured by his promise, but didn't admit as much. She didn't want him to know how much of an effect he was having on her.

"You're very astute. It is a lie, but I'm your guide here, I'm not about to tell you how my magic works. That's not the kind of thing that's approved by my people."

Macey scowled. She didn't like secret keeping, even if her gut was telling her she could trust this man and he wouldn't do anything to harm her or her men.

"Tell me what's going on here."

"I'm not sure, the lampads magic is strong, but this much? I think it must be a combination of what they can do, and your own powers as a Warden. But then, you're not just any Warden, are you?"

Macey didn't answer. Air had warned her not to

reveal her presence to anyone who didn't need to know about it and had hinted that the consequences of doing so would be dire. She didn't want to risk those things coming to pass. After all the work they'd done, she didn't want it destroyed by a moment of weakness.

Turning away, she strode back up the balustrade and looked down on the writhing mass below.

"Make them stop," she commanded.

"I can't, only you can," Luc answered.

Macey looked back over her shoulder and at Jared. "Make them stop?"

He held up his cuffed hands, a blank look on his face. "It's not me making it happen, little kelpie. My powers are as bound as yours were."

Macey's face fell. How was she supposed to stop all this if she had no idea what to do.

Closing her eyes, she willed the people below to stop what they were doing and disappear. Tingles flooded her body and flowed away from her. Slowly, she opened her eyes again.

She gasped. "But..."

"I told you," Luc said. "You are the only one who can control things here. These are your tests after all."

"Then you can't be here. None of you." Panic coloured her tone as she remembered what everyone had told her about not accepting any help in the lampads tests.

Luc laughed again. That was becoming infuriating. He needed to stop with the inappropriate laughter. "No one said this was the test they'll ask of you. It's just their magic."

"You don't know that for sure," she snapped.

"No, he doesn't," Cam responded. "Daimon's only ever have one charge. He'll have been waiting for you to turn up for years."

"You know too much," Luc muttered.

"In this case, from a daimon I used to know. She..."

"She?" Macey demanded, quiet rage beginning to fill her again.

Cam's face reddened.

"It meant nothing. It was three hundred years ago..."

"I don't care if it was a millennia ago."

"Macey, please, can we do this later?" Cam asked.

"That depends, am I suddenly going to come across *her* when I'm least expecting it?" she snapped.

"Unlikely. She'll have died with her charge."

Macey crossed her arms, looking out on the empty space rather than back at him. She hated the images that had flooded her mind and taken over her conscious. She knew her men had lives before her, she'd faced that with Rónàn. But it didn't make the idea of it any easier.

"Carry on about daimons," she instructed, still refusing to look at him.

"Even if Lucien has been this close to the lampads his whole life, he'd never have seen them in action. That's not how daimons work."

"Right, so..."

"He's correct," Luc acknowledged. "I've never seen the lampads magic in action before. But I do know more about it than most, we both have the same place of origin after all."

"Greece?"

"Yes."

"So, what happens now?" Macey asked.

"I'll guide you down the path you need and help you where I can. But I can't interfere, just like the others can't. And there will be a point where you must continue alone. You'll have to face your fate alone."

"Her fate, or the Fates?" Rónàn muttered so softly, she almost missed it.

"Just her fate," Luc confirmed. "There's been no sign of the Fates for thousands of years. They disappeared with the downfall of the Greek Empire, just like everything else save for a few stragglers. But that's hardly surprising, things are the same here.

Your Celtic gods vanished with their fall, leaving only kelpies, wraiths and other beings behind."

"The gods were real?" Macey stuttered. She'd grown up her entire life with the belief they were nothing more than the beings created by humans to explain odd occurrences.

"Of course they were once. Now... I don't think so. They abandoned Earth and left it to be the playground of their creations."

She tried to process what he was saying, but failed. It just didn't make sense with what she knew. And yet, it didn't feel like Lucien was lying to her. Far from it. Truth echoed through his words, filling the empty room far more completely than the writhing mass had.

The gods.

Even if they were dead and gone, the implications of them having existed were unthinkable.

And complicated.

As if Macey needed more of that.

FOUR

"So, what happens now?" Macey asked. "You said you were going to lead us down some kind of path?"

The daimon sighed. "I was speaking figuratively. I have no idea what actual path to take here."

"I thought this was your home?" Jared asked, eyeing his cuffs in disgust.

"It is, but it doesn't usually look like this. There are... less people. A lot less people. None at all, to be precise."

"Then where do they all come from?"

Luc shrugged. "The magic of this place is ancient, and I don't think anyone knows how it works. I just hope it takes them all away once you're gone. I like my solitude." He gestured towards the space where the people had been before and seemed to have reappeared.

Macey scowled. That was somewhat inconvenient. At least it meant it wasn't actually her test.

If this daimon wasn't going to lead them, then Macey was going to have to do it herself. Giving Luc an evil glare, she walked past him and down a muddy path towards the revellers. Most of them were naked by now, and the noise of their moans and groans was deafening. Jared appeared next to her, and she took his hand when she saw his expression. This had to be incredibly hard for the incubus.

"If I didn't know any better, I'd think that this is a test for me," he whispered. "One I'd be failing without these cuffs."

"Maybe Malan was wrong," Macey mused. "Maybe it's not me being tested. Maybe it's all of us, to prove that we're worthy to see the lampads. Or maybe this is just a coincidence." She sighed. "I really wish we had someone who told us what was happening in clear, easy to understand words. Instead, we have a prophet who likes to allude to things but never actually explains, and a daimon guide who isn't much better at giving out information."

Jared grinned. "Being a Warden sucks. All work, no rewards."

Behind them, the daimon cleared his throat.

"Being together should be reward enough. Not everyone has a relationship as loving and rewarding as yours." There was bitterness in his voice, a lot of it. Macey almost felt sorry for him. It sounded like he was lonely.

"Want to join?" a melodious voice asked from their right. A woman, her supple breasts exposed and covered in some sort of sticky liquid that looked like chocolate, was lying on the muddy ground, her legs spread. A man was... well, he was sucking her off, his head squeezed between her thighs.

"No, we're good," Macey muttered and hurried on. She wasn't sure if they really had to walk through this hedonistic village, but there was no other path, and why would the magic show them this if it wasn't relevant?

She squeezed Jared's hand tighter when she noticed him staring at the woman.

"It's going to be fine," she whispered. "Try not to look at them."

He groaned in response. "I can feel their energy," he admitted. "I can't feed off it, but I can still feel it. It's very distracting."

Macey didn't even want to imagine how it had to feel for him. Waves, even she was noticing the sexual energy in the air, and she wasn't an incubus. It had to be hell for him. Or heaven, had he been without the shackles.

She increased her pace, trying to get them away from this orgy as quickly as possible. There had to be a point to it all. They could have gone to a random brothel if they wanted to see naked people having fun with each other.

Finally, the houses became more scattered and the end of the cavern came into view. The walls were glistening with moisture, reminding Macey of... well, other moist things. She shook her head, trying to get the images out of her mind.

"There's an archway, just like the one before," Cam called from behind them, his superior senses once again coming in handy.

"Is it an illusion again?" Macey asked the incubus and he frowned in concentration.

"No, I think it's really just a doorway out of this cave."

She sighed in relief. Good. The sooner they got out of here, the better, although she was a little apprehensive of what they were going to stumble in next.

Cam sniffed the air. "There's a draught coming through there. It smells like the sea."

"The sea? Aren't we quite far away from that?"

Macey concentrated on her water magic. Indeed, she felt a light tug, pulling her towards the narrow gap in the cavern wall.

"I can feel it too," Rónàn confirmed. "Salt water."

Smiling at the familiar sensation, Macey stepped through the archway, her steps quickening. The tunnel was dark, but she wasn't as scared of stumbling as she had been before. The sea was waiting for her. Water, proper clean water, not like the Thames water they'd seen outside. Maybe this was some kind of underground estuary?

Faster and faster she walked, dragging Jared with her.

Water.

Then, suddenly, the ground stopped and there was nothing there, just air, and she fell, screaming.

Time slowed down as she saw the glowing walls of a new cave, reflecting on the surface of the water far below them... but it was coming closer, fast, and then they crashed into it, sinking quickly.

Without even thinking about it, Macey shifted. It was probably the fastest she had ever changed into her kelpie form, but it was also one of the most painful shifts ever. Her bones hurt where they'd lengthened and thickened, and even her scalp was throbbing. She breathed in the icy water, her gills filtering it.

It tasted amazing. Salty, refreshing, pure. Unbelievable pure for being under such a large, polluted city.

She flicked her tail through the water, her mood changing to playfulness. This was a place she was going to be able to have some fun. Rónàn might want to join her in a long, drawn out swim. She focused on her antenna sense, searching for other people in the water. It was only her and Jared so far, the others must have been able to stop.

Jared. Oh no. She swam towards the incubus who was sinking ever lower, unmoving. She gently took his arm between her jaws, shaking him. No response. She had to get him out of the water. Incubi couldn't breathe underwater. The kelpie in her found that very strange, but her human self was still strong enough to realise how important it was to get Jared to the surface.

She gripped his sleeve with her teeth and pulled him up, swimming as fast as she could. They'd drifted down further than she'd realised. The water was dark, almost black, but she knew where the surface was. She was a kelpie, after all.

When her head broke the surface, she brought her legs underneath Jared's body, lifting him up until he was lying on his back, his face in the air. He wasn't breathing.

Fuck.

She wasn't going to be able to shift while holding him above the surface of the water. How was she supposed to help him? Revive him?

She whinnied in distress, the sound echoing

through the cave, making it sound as if there was a whole army of kelpies standing around her.

"Coming!" a voice called from far above, and a moment later, a body crashed into the water beside her, spraying her with water. Her eyes were beginning to dry out, not used to being exposed to air, so she lowered her head beneath the surface, taking a deep breath.

It was Rónàn, shirtless and with bare feet, swimming towards her. He was so much better prepared than she had been. Oh well, it was her who'd discovered this lake... kind of, so of course she'd been surprised by the fall and the water.

The selkie surfaced, taking in a deep breath, then immediately took over from Macey, holding Jared's head. He put his ear against the incubus's chest, listening for a heart beat.

He smiled and nodded at Macey when he found it, then pressed his lips against Jared's, breathing into his mouth.

This was the second time now that those two were kissing. Well, this time it was a kiss of life, but still. At least this time, there was no jealousy in Macey's heart.

She shifted back as quickly as she'd changed into her kelpie form, the anxiety over Jared's fate making the pain pale into insignificance.

She thought about begging Rónàn to work faster,

to save him, but she knew it wouldn't make a difference. The selkie wouldn't skip on saving Jared. He cared about Macey and their family unit too much. She just hoped that his selkie magic was enough to save her incubus. Tears slipped down her face, unnoticed through the salt water itself.

"What's happening?" Cam shouted down from the ledge above.

She didn't answer, but relief filled her just by knowing that she didn't have to save two of them.

Air buffeted the water, causing ripples to cascade over the surface. Macey looked away, not really wanting her eyes to dry out too much. That would make re-submerging them painful and she had no desire for that to be the case.

"Let me take him back to the land," Luc requested.

Macey shook her head.

"What good would that do? Obviously we need to be down here."

"Or maybe this is just another test. This doesn't work unless you trust me."

Her eyes met those of the daimon as Rónàn continued to try saving Jared.

"Prove it."

"How would you like me to do that? This isn't the best place to doubt anyone," Luc pointed out.

"Remove the cuffs," she demanded, only realising

as she finished speaking that it might be just what they needed to save his life.

"I don't think..."

"I can't feel any of the sexual energy from the village, it's safe for now."

"He still needs to have them on, Macey, please trust me."

"So you keep saying, but so far you've done nothing to actually prove I can," she snapped. "It's all just words. Nothing more than words."

Indecision warred over his face.

"Let me take him back to land, and then I'll remove his cuffs."

Macey glanced at her two men, but saw no change in Jared's status. All that seemed to be happening was Rónàn growing weaker. Much as she was. While it was easy to stay afloat in her kelpie form, her human one wasn't nearly so resilient and she could feel the burn in her legs and arms just from treading water.

"Very well," she accepted.

Rónàn ceased what he was doing and pushed on Jared's limp form to help Luc take him into his arms. With the man settled, Luc flapped his wings and soared upwards, apparently not suffering at all from the weight of another man on him.

Macey closed the gap between the two of them left in the water. Rónàn slipped an arm around her, pulling her closer. She appreciated the gesture and support, leaning on him. She really was lucky to find the men she had.

Luc returned moments later and held out his hand to Macey. "You need to be up there too."

"And Rónàn?" she asked, without accepting.

"I'll return for him in a moment, but I think you'll be more useful to the incubus."

She nodded and allowed the daimon to hoist her out of the water. She tried not to think about the fact shifting had left her without any clothing and the daimon could see her naked. His wings moved the air around her in a way which had her stomach dropping. She didn't like being in the air. She'd discovered that with Cam before and hadn't been in any rush to repeat the experience. But she knew Jared was more important than her hatred of flying.

Luc set her down and she stumbled slightly, only staying upright by falling into Cam's arms.

"One cuff free incubus," Luc muttered, waving his hand in Jared's direction. The cuffs unclicked and fell to the dirt floor. "Don't lose them, you will need them."

"Can't you just make more when that happens?" Cam asked.

Luc fixed him with a disbelieving look. "What do you think I am? I can't make things out of thin air, you know. I have to have them on me anyway."

"Please just go get Rónàn," Macey begged, her

worries resting with her selkie down below. She couldn't have been the only one to be tiring and she didn't want to swap one man in danger for another one.

"As my lady commands." Luc gave the most ridiculous bow, but Macey didn't care, she just rushed over to Jared, falling to her knees and pressing her head against his chest. A faint heartbeat reached her ears and she almost yelled in relief. He was alive.

"How do we..." she started to ask. But the moment her eyes fell on Cam, she knew the answer.

And so did he, if the way he was unbuttoning his shirt was anything to go by.

"I know," he whispered.

Macey rose to her feet and closed the gap between them. While she longed to savor this time with Cam, she knew it wasn't going to be an option. It was a good job he knew every button she could press.

"I hope this works," she admitted.

"It should do," Cam replied, though his voice shook, revealing just how worried he was about his friend.

She closed the gap between them, pressing her naked body against his. He circled her in his arms, pulling her closer so he could lower his lips to hers.

Cam's kiss was searing. Desperate. Consuming. Like

her, he was only half there as he worried about his friend, but she was okay with that. This wasn't about intimacy between them, though she was sure it'd be enjoyable. Their focus was on recharging Jared's powers and saving him from the coma like state he'd fallen into.

Carefully, Cam laid Macey down on the floor, neither of them caring for the dirt that littered it. Their eyes met and Macey saw the love and devotion in his gaze. He wasn't just doing this for Jared. Cam was doing this for her too.

She cupped his cheek in her hand before kissing him again, their worry and concern turning into a deep passion. Cam loved her, just as the others did, and even if the circumstances were dire, he'd take this opportunity to show her just how much.

Without waiting, Cam thrust inside her, his cock filling her completely. Macey groaned, throwing her head back and pushing her body against his. The worries fled her mind as she lost herself in the sensations of Cam inside her and his kisses peppering her neck.

They weren't taking their time as they usually did. This was a quick, hard, intense love making, but hopefully it would be enough for Jared.

The sound of wings behind them almost made Macey look up, but she really didn't want to face the daimon in the naked and sweaty state she was in.

Hopefully, he'd do the decent thing and look away, or better, fly far away, giving them some space.

"Do you need me as well?" Rónàn asked just when Cam thrust hard into Macey and she moaned heavily.

"Check on Jared," she gasped. Cam was gripping her breasts now, twirling her nipples between his fingers. She loved it when he did that.

"His heartbeat is stronger now," Rónàn reported. "I think it's working."

That spurned Cam on and his thrusts became harder, quicker, until Macey was a moaning mess, writhing on the stone floor, her hands grasping for something to hold on to. She found Rónàn's ankles and gripped them tight.

He didn't comment on it, but when she looked up, the heat in his eyes was almost overwhelming to watch.

She was unravelling fast and wasn't going to last much longer. Cam was pounding into her, his groans becoming louder.

"Jared?" she asked but it came out as a moan.

"Getting stronger," Rónàn confirmed. "His breathing has steadied."

One more thrust, one more twirl of her nipples, and Macey couldn't hold it together anymore. She came apart, screaming as the orgasm ripped through her. This was intense, strangely amplified by their surroundings and the worry for the incubus. She was shaking, still holding on to Rónàn's ankles as Cam came within her, gripping her thighs tighter than was comfortable. She didn't mind. She was looking into his eyes, the love and passion in them obvious. She hoped he'd see the same in hers. They were made for each other, all five of them, even though Flint wasn't here with them.

With a sudden gasp, Jared sat up, sucking in a deep breath.

"What...?"

His voice was hoarse and shaky.

Macey let go of Rónàn's ankles and the selkie moved back to Jared's side.

"You almost drowned," he explained. "Cam and Macey have been... ehm... feeding you."

Jared turned around, his movements slow. His eyes widened when he saw the two of them naked and on the floor, their skin covered in dust.

"Oh," was all he said. "Thanks."

Cam slid out of Macey and got up.

"How are you feeling, mate?"

"Okay, I guess," Jared said. "I think I need another meal to be fully back to my old strength."

Macey was exhausted from the quick fuck with Cam, but she smiled at the incubus nonetheless. "I volunteer."

He shook his head. "No, not now. We need to go

on, I can feel a disturbance in the earth. We shouldn't linger here."

They all stared at him.

"A disturbance?" Macey finally asked. "What do you mean?"

Cam passed her his shirt and she slipped it on, thankful he was tall enough that it fell past her ass and at least gave her some cover.

The loud whoosh of wings announced Luc's arrival before he landed on the stone ledge a second later.

"He means we need to leave, now."

The urgency in his voice had Macey getting up immediately. She started to put her clothes back on, wishing she could take a shower first. Cam was already half dressed, hiding the view of his perfect abs. Later, she promised herself. Jared was going to need another meal, and maybe he was wanting to take part in it too. And maybe Rónàn too... was she being greedy?

"Cuffs back on, incubus," Luc warned and handed them to Jared.

"Is that really necessary?" Macey asked but Jared had already clicked them around his wrists. He still looked pale and weak, but if what he'd said was true, they needed to move.

"How are we getting off here?" Rónàn asked. "Do we jump down again and swim?"

Luc sighed. "The path continues on the other side of the cave. I'll fly you there, one by one. You can thank me later."

Without warning, he grabbed Macey, even though she still hadn't put on her jacket again, and took her into the air with him.

She disliked the daimon more and more. Even Malan was preferable to him.

When they were halfway above the lake, Luc whispered into Macey's ear, "I won't be getting the others. From here on, you have to go alone."

It took a moment for his words to register.

"No, you can't do that!" she protested, her voice almost a scream. "Get them now!"

"You may not trust me, but I'm your daimon," he said coldly. "I know what's best for you."

"You bleeding don't!" she shouted. "We need to stick together!"

"No, you don't. The lampads will not show themselves as long as the men are with you. You do want to rescue your Fire Warden, don't you?"

"But..." The protest was ripped from Macey's throat when Luc let her go and she fell the last three feet onto hard ground. They were on another stone ledge, the only way forwards a narrow tunnel. This one was different though, it looked more planned and precise, less natural. There were rough chisel marks on the walls. Someone had built this tunnel.

"Now go," Luc said, his voice suddenly filled with urgency. "Something is coming for your men and if they know you're waiting over here, they won't leave."

"Just fly them here!" Macey demanded, but the daimon had already flown away into the darkness.

She groaned in frustration.

"Jared!" she screamed, hoping her voice would echo through the cavern. "Rónàn! Cam!"

There was no response, no matter how hard she listened. The water down below seemed to suck up all the sounds. She was alone.

Illustration: Lampad

FIVE

S he stared at the other side for another moment, but saw and heard nothing.

"Guess I really am doing this alone," she muttered.

As much as she didn't like it, she also knew Luc was right. She had to do this bit alone. She'd known from the beginning that the lampads weren't going to give her anything if she didn't do this alone. Though she had hoped that she'd be able to have her men with her up until the last moment.

Trusting herself, she turned her back on the cliff her men still stood on and made her way down the path. The salt smell of the sea disappeared as quickly as it had come, leaving a pang of longing in its place. She missed having water around her, but that was nothing new. She was glad her men had a house with a swimming pool she could use, otherwise leaving the water for them would be torture, no matter how much she loved them.

A chill stole over her and sent shivers down her spine. That wasn't right. She didn't feel the cold, it was part of her kelpie nature. Which could only mean one thing. It wasn't natural. But it also didn't make sense, the lampads were fire creatures, they shouldn't be making her feel so cold. It just made no sense.

She turned a corner, the small, tight path not getting any wider. Shadows flickered against the walls, though Macey wasn't sure what caused them. While she could see, she couldn't work out where the light was coming from. Considering she was magical herself, she was really starting to dislike everything else to do with it.

Another corner came, but around this one, she found the first evidence of flames, though these ones were eerie blue and filled the hall with creepy light. Macey found she preferred the mystery from before.

"Hello?" she called out.

All she got was crackles in return. She scowled. That wasn't what she'd had in mind.

"My name is Macey," she shouted. "I'm the Water Warden. I've come seeking your assistance in a matter of great importance," she added, hoping it would spur the lampads on to appear rather than just doing their vague fire thing. It just wasn't a good sign.

She stepped forward again, the path finally opening up into a wider room. The whole place was carved into stone, but there was nothing natural about it. This was a place made by man or magic. Macey would put her money on the latter of the two. The fires still crackled, echoing around the room as they increased in their ferocity.

"Please, I've come here for your help, to submit to whatever test you wish to give me." And she was really fed up with all the cryptic magical nonsense.

A fire spurted up from the ground, causing Macey to jump backwards to avoid being burned. The brightness ebbed away, leaving a writhing woman in the flames. No. Not in the flames. The woman was made of them. Her whole body a crackling swirling mass of sparks. If Macey hadn't been able to see it with her own eyes, then she'd never have believed it to be possible.

Which was a little idiotic given she'd seen people made of clouds before.

"Hello?" she asked again, nerves cracking her voice and revealing her apprehension.

"Hello, Macey. Warden of Water." The voice didn't sound like one person, but like a chorus of voices all singing in unison.

"I'm here seeking an audience with the lampads."

"Then you've come to the right place," the woman answered.

"Are you one?"

"No, I am but an apparition. I am the gatekeeper to the lampads."

"May I see them?" she asked, confused but determined.

"Not yet. You must pass a test first."

"I thought I didn't have to pass any tests until they knew what I wanted?" She cocked her head to the side and tried to discern the fire woman's expression.

"That is true. But you may not see them without passing a test first."

"I've had enough of bloody tests," Macey muttered to herself. "Tell me what I must do," she directed at the fire-woman.

"In order to reach the lampads, you must pass through the tunnel of fire."

"Okay." Macey nodded, not wanting to admit how terrifying that sounded. She might be a being of water, but she imagined that magical fire could still burn her. And if it did...well, it wouldn't be as easy to heal her as it was to heal Jared.

"The entrance is to your left, Water Warden. You may not use magic. You must not stop. You must not answer any of the calls."

Dread flowed through Macey at the instructions.

What could she be about to face if that was the list of things she couldn't do.

"I understand," she acknowledged.

"Then proceed." The fire-woman lifted her arm and waved to the entrance, which turned out to be nothing more than another cave entrance.

The main difference was that this cave was covered in a ring of fire. One Macey knew she'd have to step through.

"Thank you for your guidance."

"You're welcome, Water Warden."

Macey nodded, but said nothing else. She stepped towards the cave, her heart pounding in her throat. She didn't want to be scared, but there was a part of her that was. She didn't know what lay in wait for her beyond this cave and from the sound of it, she didn't want to either.

The heat batted against her skin as she stepped through the entrance. She closed her eyes, mustering up all of the courage she could.

The flames were even hotter within and she tried to ignore the overbearing heat of it all.

Before her, the flames began to rise, forming shapes within them. Shapes she recognised.

An orca dived between a sea of fire waves. A beithir flew high above. Selkies, cat-sith...just about every other creature she'd met on her journey appeared in the flames.

While she longed to stop and see what else she could spot, she knew she had to ignore them. They weren't real. They were just apparitions sent to distract her from her purpose.

"Macey!" someone called.

She ignored it.

"Macey!" another voice called.

She swallowed hard. She recognised those voices. She knew them as well as she knew her own. She tried to ignore them. She tried to remind herself they weren't real, but the voices continued to shout and she wanted to answer them. She'd never ignored her men's pleas before. It didn't feel right to do that now.

"Macey!" This time, it was Amber's voice calling, but she didn't sound in distress. She sounded gloating. "Macey!" she called again, drawing out her name.

Knowing she had to ignore it, Macey carried on down her path, one step after another, her focus on getting to the other side and meeting the lampads.

"Your fate was so tragic," Amber called. "Died trying to save one of the people you loved. It's a shame you weren't enough. But that just left more for me. All we had to do was invest someone else as the Water Warden. So easy to replace." Amber's voice came out like a sneer, and unlike any Amber Macey had ever encountered.

She ignored her, even as jealousy tugged within her. She knew she wasn't as easily replaced as that, either in her men's hearts, or in her position as one of the Seven Wardens. She also knew Amber was far too happy with her mage to go after Macey's men for herself. The beithir just wasn't that way inclined.

"Our hearts were easily given again," Cam's voice came. "We've shared before, we'll share again. Sharing with Izban is a small price to pay for someone's love."

"I had to do it, Macey. Losing you was too much for me to take. I'm an incubus, I need someone who is always going to be there to sate me. And you weren't. You were too busy saving another man for my needs. Amber is everything I truly need and desire."

"She sparked my flame to life," Flint joined in. "Not like your water dousing flames. She can create them."

Macey's gut twisted in on itself as she listened to the cat-calls of the fake apparitions. They just wanted to stop her on her journey. The lampads had chosen their test well. It sent needles of pain through her heart unlike any she'd ever experienced before. There was no way she could ignore this, and yet she knew she had to.

A tear splashed onto the floor and gave a hiss as it evaporated into the air. The heat was crazy and Macey was surprised it hadn't burned through her shoes and clothing already.

If this was the test just to meet the lampads, then she dreaded to think what they had in store for her once they heard what she wanted.

"I was never sure if you loved me as much as the others. I came in later after all. And I'm not a Warden. It was easy for me to accept that role. I'm another water being after all. And with me as the Water Warden, with Amber at the centre, we can be Wardens in truth," Rónàn sneered.

Another tear fell.

"Why did you have to leave?" Izban demanded. "Now I have to share the woman I love. You left, and now she has everyone and everything. Yet another thing you ruined for me."

"Ruined?" Cam laughed. "It's hardly ruined. Everything is how it was meant to be. The Wardens are one in spirit as well as in body."

"I'm sorry, Macey. Please forgive me," Jared begged. "I had no choice. It was this or die myself and the world needs the Wardens."

"I did consider returning to the selkies, but then Amber visited me at night. We..."

Macey clapped her hands over her ears, hoping to block out the sounds of their voices. Her tears were falling thick and fast as what they were saying broke through her defenses, shredding her heart to pieces over and over again. Each time she managed to remind herself she was just being tested, something else would break through her defences and shatter it over and over again.

If the lampads couldn't help her, then she was going to be left broken and shattered. A shell of her past self.

"Macey, don't listen, you're nearly there." Luc's voice was soft and reassuring.

She looked up to find the daimon's figure in the flames. His expression was one of pity. She hoped it was just another part of the magic and not something he could actually witness and react to.

She said nothing, knowing she couldn't or she would fail.

Some things were more important than her broken heart. And this was one of them.

She took a deep breath, almost searing her throat in the process because the air was so hot, and ran, ignoring the voices, holding her heart pieces together as best as she could. Letting go was not an option. She felt like she was about to fall apart and that would have meant the end of not just her, but of Flint as well. Even if he was with Amber... no. He wasn't. It was all just a trick, an illusion created to throw her off her path. If she didn't complete this quest, he might never recover, and without their Fire Warden, their fight against the Mahoun and his siblings was looking bleak. This was more important than just her.

She squeezed her eyes shut when more people

appeared in the flames. Nessie, shouting something about being Macey's mother. Yes, she already knew that, it wasn't news. Didn't mean she had to accept it, though.

Suddenly, something tripped her and she fell to the ground, screaming as her hands touched the scorching earth. Flames licked on her skin, blisters forming immediately. It hurt, hurt so much, but the physical pain also helped block out the mental agony she was still feeling.

She jumped back to her feet, noticing that she was almost at the end of the fire tunnel. She stumbled the last few metres, her hands hurting like hell. Maybe this was hell. The fire certainly fit. She had trouble believing that she was really still underneath London. Maybe there had been some weird portal that they hadn't even noticed. Maybe it had been the archways that had led them into the strange cave full of naked people. She grimaced. Compared to this fire torture, that hadn't been all that bad.

As soon as the fire stopped and she was standing in cool, fresh air, she came to a halt, looking at her burned hands. They were red and covered in tiny blisters, some of them oozing already. This was going to need some attention soon, before she got an infection.

"Who are you, what do you want and why aren't you dead?"

A booming voice suddenly came from all around her. It was neither male nor female, but something in between.

There was nobody to be seen. It was another cave, bare and empty, not particularly big. Behind her, the flames were slowly flickering out, revealing the long, dark tunnel she'd come through. Well, thanks. They couldn't have stopped burning while she was running through it, could they.

Macey was getting tired of caves. Really, really tired.

"I'm Macey, I'm the Water Warden and I'm looking for the lampads," she said in a clear, confident voice. Not like she felt at all, but her diplomatic training was kicking in. She'd been trained to react calmly in difficult situations.

"How did you enjoy the fire, little water being?"

The voice was mocking her, but Macey refused to give in.

"I'm here for your help," she called out. "A friend of mine, the Fire Warden, is injured and needs help. If you don't want to help me because I'm representing water, fine, but please help him!"

Silence greeted her words.

"Hello?" she asked. Still, no response. The voice had disappeared.

She took a deep breath and tried to block out the agonising pain in her hands. There was another tunnel leading out of this cave, so it seemed as good an option as any. Waiting for a few more seconds for the voice to return, she moved to the tunnel entrance and peeked inside. There was only darkness, except for a single flickering flame at the very end.

"Hello?" she called into the tunnel, her voice echoing slightly.

Unsurprisingly, nobody answered. She sighed. These lampads really didn't like visitors.

Gathering her courage, she began to walk into the tunnel. It was even narrower than the ones before and she was almost glad that her men weren't with her. They wouldn't have fit.

The flame came closer and closer. When Macey finally stumbled out of the tunnel, she was in, guess what, yet another cave.

This one was bigger than the last, and illuminated by hundreds of flames floating in the air, not just the one she'd seen from afar. There were no people though, just the flames.

"Hello?" she called out for the third time.

"Welcome, Daughter of Water," a voice said, different from the one before, but just as sexless. "We have been waiting for you."

Macey was tempted to respond with a sarcastic 'it didn't seem that way', but she kept her mouth shut.

"I'm here for your help," she said instead, repeating her request.

"Yes, we know him, the Son of Fire," the voice said. "He is suffering a great deal."

Her heart threatened to break apart yet again. "Can you help him?"

"We could."

She waited for an explanation, but none came. "Yes? Could you? Please?"

"We don't just help anyone." The voice sighed, as if that was supposed to be obvious. "You will have to prove that he is worthy."

"Wait, that *he* is worthy? How am I supposed to do that?"

"Tell us about him."

Macey thought for a moment. "Well, he's a wraith, he wields fire magic, he's one of the Seven Wardens, he's-"

"No," the voice interrupted her, a chiding tone vibrating in it. "Tell us about him, about how you see him. We don't need to know about his life. We want to know about his soul."

"Oh," Macey muttered, trying to rearrange her thoughts. If only her hands weren't hurting so much. The pain was making concentrating rather hard.

"He's kind, he's strong, he's generous. He likes to help others. He's got a great sense of humour. I love it when he laughs, he gets little dimples on his cheeks..."

She let her voice trail off, certain that this was not what the lampads wanted to hear.

"Continue."

The command surprised her. Apparently she was going in the right direction.

"He likes to tickle me," she admitted, a little embarrassed. "And sometimes, when we're alone, he tells me secrets. I think he does it more for himself than for me. You know, he wants to get things off his chest so they don't hurt him anymore. He's lived for a long time, but he's refusing to tell me his exact age. A lot of things have happened during his lifetime, and sometimes he gets sad, even though I don't know why. He gets that look in his eyes..."

She stopped, anger suddenly bubbling up in her. "Is that enough now? Have I told you enough about him? I don't know if it's your place to know all this. It should be him telling you things like that, not me."

"You're loyal," the voice observed. "Do you love him?"

Macey didn't have to think about that. "Yes, I do."

"Would you die for him?"

The impassioned voice made it hard for Macey to get a feel for it. Was this a threat? Did this mean she'd have to die to save Flint?

"I probably would, yes," she said, "but other people are relying on me, on all of us. We're the

Wardens, we need to fix the world. We can't just give up, we need to keep on fighting."

"Probably isn't good enough," the voice said with a tone of disappointment. "You need to be sure."

"I am sure!" Macey shouted, scared they might not take her seriously. "I love him! What else do you want? I would die for him, I want him to live, I never want to lose him, and I want him to have his magic back. Is that so hard to understand?"

"It isn't, child." The voice was suddenly soothing and gentle, as if someone else was speaking with the same voice. Maybe it was several people talking to her, even though it sounded like it was all the same. "We see that you want to help him."

"Then can you help me make him better?" Macey asked, desperation flooding her heart. "Because if you can't, then I'd rather return and be by his side."

"There is a way we can help," the voice said slowly. "It's not without sacrifice though."

"I'll give whatever you need," Macey replied without hesitation. "Just tell me what I need to do."

"It's simple. You will need to carry our flame to him."

That sounded too easy. She could just take a torch, light it with their flame, then take the Staran to get back to Malan's house. No, that was far too easy for these strange beings who had already tortured her just so she could get an audience.

"What's the catch?" she asked and the voice laughed.

"You will have to carry it in your hands."

Suddenly, the blisters on her skin felt as if they were exploding, agony flooding not just through her hands, but through her entire body. She looked down and saw flames circling her fingers, burning into her flesh. Were they going to burn until there was nothing left of her hands?

"Run, child," the voice called to her. "Run and bring him the flame. There's an entrance to the Staran at the end of this cave. Run and get there before the flame has nothing left to feed from."

Macey wanted to cry, to cower on the ground and somehow extinguish the flames that were hurting her, but Flint's face was burning in her mind, encouraging her, showing her why she was doing this. She had to help him. He was worth it. The pain wouldn't matter once she'd given the lampad's fire to him.

She ran, more stumbling than actually running, towards the other side of the cave. A simple door was cut into the stone. She hesitated for a moment, then pressed her burning hands against it. She screamed as the pain became worse than ever, but the door opened, giving way to the swirling fogs of the Staran. She stepped forward and thought of Malan's house, willing the Staran to carry her there.

SIX

She landed with a thud as the Staran threw her out. She cupped her hands together, hoping she'd done enough to keep the flame alive. The last thing she wanted was to end up with nothing to rekindle Flint's magic with.

She got to her feet, trying not to stumble, but it was difficult with her hands occupied. But she needed to get into Malan's house. To get to Flint and save him from the lack of magic.

She pushed through the front door, ignoring all the people who tried to talk to her. None of them had any right to stop her from reaching Flint and doing what she needed to.

Rushing through the hallway to Flint's room, her foot caught and she fell to the floor. She held her hands to catch her fall, only realising what that would mean seconds before they touched the floor. She closed her fists tightly, hoping it would protect the flame currently burning in her left hand.

She rolled, panic building inside her. She didn't dare to open her and see the fate of the flame. She just needed to get it to Flint and do... well, she wasn't all that sure what she needed to do. The lampads hadn't told her any of that and she hadn't thought to ask. Though given their attitude, she doubted they'd have given her the answers she needed.

Back on her feet, she kicked open the door to Flint's room and half-ran straight to Flint's bed side.

His eyes were closed and his skin pale, he was just a shadow of his former self and it scared her. She hated thinking this had happened because of her. But she was doing something about it now. It had to work.

Not knowing what to do, she pressed her hands against Flint's heart, flattening them against his chest and willing the flames to jump into him. To do something.

Silently, she begged for some sign that her plan had worked.

But nothing came.

Flint didn't move. Not even a flutter of his eyelids.

She was too late.

Slowly, Macey lifted her hands and turned them over, expecting to see the flame lingering there still.

She stared at them in horror, before her gaze flickered to Flint's chest.

No flame there either.

What could have happened to it?

She willed the flame to reappear, but all that happened was the blisters on her hands starting to burn and pulse. She could have sworn they started to glow too, but that couldn't be right.

"Macey?" a female voice asked.

She swung her head around, registering that it was Amber talking to her.

Amber...

The cruel taunts from her trip through the flames trickled back into her mind, reminding her of how the other woman was ready to take her place.

Rage built up inside her, taking over every fibre of her being.

"Macey, are you okay?" Concern marred the redhead's features, but that barely registered in Macey's anger-fuelled brain.

"You," she hissed. "How *dare* you think you can replace me?"

"Replace you? What are you-"

"Don't think to deny it," Macey countered. "I know all of your plans."

"I don't have any plans. Macey, what happened? Where are the others?"

Macey didn't answer, instead, she fixed her hatred-filled gaze on the other woman. This person wanted her men. She wanted to take her place. At this point, it wouldn't surprise Macey to discover *she* was the one to steal Flint's magic in an attempt to steal the power.

"Get out," Macey hissed.

Amber didn't need to be told twice and scrambled from her seat. She was probably running to her mage. Izban wouldn't be able to save her from Macey's wrath. No one could.

Macey glanced back at Flint's still and lifeless body. Inwardly, she could feel the tears that wanted to fall, but something within her wouldn't let them go. She couldn't allow the pain to take over. Not when she had her anger to sate.

Without wasting another moment on the dead, she stormed back out of the room and through Malan's house, paying as little attention to the people around her as she had when she'd come in.

She slammed the front door closed behind her and ran into the middle of the field in front of the house. Macey fell to her knees, bruising them as she did, and let out a keening scream. All her rage, all her pain, all her fury, let loose in one loud scream. She could have been mistaken for a *bean sí* with the noise she was making. Maybe becoming one of the heralds of death would be preferable to this torture.

"MACEY!" Amber called out.

Macey got to her feet, spurred on by the hatred bubbling in every part of her. The woman was behind her. And she wasn't alone. Macey didn't need to turn around to know that. How *dare* she bring back up. She thought she was so much better than Macey. She thought she could take Macey's place. And yet, she needed other people to help take Macey down.

She spun, throwing her hands up and feeling power crackle around them. It felt different from her water magic, but she didn't question that in her rage. Nor did she pay any attention to the small part within reminding her that none of what the voices said was true. That none of what had happened was Amber's fault, and even if it was, it would have been an accident.

Her eyes hardened as she stared at Amber and Izban. Some of the other assembled beings were flanking them, but she didn't focus long enough to figure out who they were.

"How *dare* you try to take them from me!" she shouted, her gaze burning through them all.

Amber tried to speak, but Macey shushed her in a motion, a crackle of flames following after her hand. That should have been enough to stop her. To calm her and make her stop, but she didn't want to. She wanted to get rid of the rage inside her. Unleash it and let it destroy everything around them all. Why should anyone be happy when she was left like this.

Flames leaped from her hands and into the dry grass, singeing and burning everything in its path. She should call it back into her and stop this madness. But the time for should had passed. Now was the time for retribution.

"Macey!" Flint's voice called.

How cruel was her mind. Reminding her of the voice of her dead love. She willed the voice to go away. To leave her be in her grief.

"Macey! Stop!"

No. She refused to listen to the phantom. He was gone. he couldn't be talking to her, advising her, helping her. She closed her eyes against the chance of seeing him. She didn't need any more torture than she was already enduring.

"Macey, please?" he begged, his voice closer this time. "You're going to hurt someone."

"Only those who deserve it," she spat out.

"No one here has done anything to deserve your anger, Macey. Please listen to me."

"Why should I listen to you? You're dead and gone. You've abandoned me." Her anger waned every so slightly, but only to be replaced by sadness and regret.

"Dead? I'm not dead. You saved me."

"I saw you dead," she countered. "Don't do this to me, Flint."

"I'm not doing anything."

Hands slipped around her and she tried to fight them off. Who was conjuring such visions? Making her think Flint was with her again? It was despicable magic. Vile. Whoever it was should be burned. She could arrange that. All it would take is a flick of the wrist.

"Macey, please open your eyes?" Flint begged, his voice low and soft in her ear.

"No, you're not real. I can't do it. I can't face it." She shook her head furiously.

"I promise you, I'm real. you can see me and touch me."

"How do I know it isn't just some vile trick? To force me into submission."

"You just have to trust me," he whispered. "But I can help you with the flames. You don't have to let them be so out of control. Trust me, Macey, please."

Something clicked within her and she opened her eyes in time to watch the crackling flames on her hands diminish and turn into nothing more than sparks.

Slowly, she turned in the man's arms, almost

screaming when she saw it was indeed Flint holding her. He had a serious expression on his face, and still looked a little too pale for her liking, but he was with her, and he was alive. That was the main thing.

"Flint?" she whispered, her voice cracking as it returned to normal.

"Shh, I'm here, Macey. I'm real and I've got you."

She nodded and collapsed into his arms, the anger giving way into tears. The fires within her died down, along with the anger and grief. There was no need for them now. She sunk to her knees once more, still wrapped up in Flint's arms.

"I've got you, Macey. You're safe." He stroked her hair as he continued to whisper, giving her the comfort she needed.

SHE WAS HUDDLED up on the sofa, a blanket wrapped around her shoulders while a healer worked on her hands. Flint was by her side, hugging her close. Her hands hurt like hell, but the pain within her mind was much worse. She wasn't sure what to believe anymore. Flint was real, safe, healthy - wasn't he? Was this just an illusion, like the fiery visions in the tunnel of fire?

Macey was beginning to think that the flames she'd carried hadn't just hurt her hands. They'd also seared her mind, breaking open doubts and wounds she hadn't known she carried.

After the healer left, they sat in silence, both lost in thought.

"How did I wield fire?" she suddenly asked, surprising both herself and Flint. Besides the healer, they were alone in the living room. Malan had made sure of that.

"Maybe you still had some of the lampad's flames left over?"

She shook her head. "No, it was all gone. I would have felt it."

He was silent for a moment and Macey was beginning to think that he didn't have any answers either, but then he cleared his throat, hugging her even tighter.

"You know how you have markings of all seven elements?" he said quietly. "Maybe it's not just because you're connected to us. Maybe it's because you're supposed to wield all of them."

"All of them?" she repeated weakly. "How is that supposed to work? Sometimes it's hard enough to control my water magic, and Air stays quiet most of the time as well. I can't imagine having five other elements to deal with."

She shuddered at the thought. She didn't want to be special. She wanted to be just one of the Seven Wardens, no different from any of them. They didn't need a leader or someone who was more powerful than the others. No, she just wanted to stay as she was.

"Maybe I'm wrong," Flint said soothingly, probably realising how much the thought upset Macey. "It's just a theory that's been playing in my mind for awhile. You're the only one of us who's got markings. It must mean something."

"Or maybe it's just a cruel trick of nature," Macey muttered bitterly. "Just another trick or test. It's getting too much, Flint. I'm not sure how much longer I can keep doing this. Fighting impossible quests. Following vague hints. Protecting the people I love. Some days I just want to lie down and give up."

"We all do," Flint whispered. "Life isn't fair. Why can't we just be like ordinary people, not having to worry about saving the world. But we've been given this task and there's nobody else to do it. At least we're together, all of us. We've got allies, we've got friends." He chuckled softly. "Even a rogue selkie. You're at the centre of our team, Macey, and you deserve to be there. You're strong, even though you might not always feel that way."

The bitterness in her disagreed with that. She wasn't special, she wasn't strong. She was just an ordinary loch kelpie, forced to deal with things that were way out of her control.

"Once this is over, we need a holiday. Somewhere

far, far away from any trouble. Just the five of us, no prophets, no monsters, no quests. I'm so tired of it all."

He kissed her cheek. "Promise."

THEY SAT on the sofa for what felt like hours. After thinking she'd lost him, Macey couldn't let Flint go. She was hugging him close and he was doing the same to her. Even though they weren't talking, she felt like they were communicating in a deep, secret way. Their bond was getting even stronger.

Her sense of near loss almost overwhelmed her concerns for her other men. For now, those worries had to remain at the back of her mind or else she'd send herself mad.

At some point, the door opened and one of the kelpies popped his head in, mouthing whether they needed anything, but Flint shook his head and the kelpie left. Macey knew they'd have to go outside soon, talk to their allies, make plans, and eventually leave to attack the Mahoun, but for now, this was a short respite that she was going to take full advantage of.

"I'm glad you saved me," Flint whispered, his lips drawing shapes onto her cheek. "The afterlife would have been terribly boring without you."

Despite herself, she laughed. "You believe in an afterlife?"

"Of course I do. I've seen it."

She shifted away from him so she could see his face.

"You have?"

He nodded. "In my dreams. And before you say it was just a dream, Cam has seen the same thing. I think it's a wraith thing. Neither of us know any other wraiths, so maybe it isn't, but our theory is that we're somehow connected to the other spheres. That's why we can so easily travel the Staran. We're not bound to one world like other races are."

"You've never told me why it is that you don't know about your own people."

He shrugged, a trace of sadness in his eyes. "I don't remember my childhood. I have no idea who my parents are. Or if I even have any. It's the same for Cam. Both of us just have memories of the past, even one we can both pinpoint as our first, but we can't remember what happened before. How we grew up. Where we came from. Who our families are. All I know is that I'm a wraith, but most of the time, I have no idea what that entails."

"You've never talked about that," Macey said, surprised and a little shocked.

He chuckled darkly. "It's not something I like to linger on. I have Cam, Rónàn, and Jared, and you, but sometimes, I still feel lonely. Fuck, that sounds depressing." He chuckled again. "But anyway, yes, there's an afterlife, and it's not all that bad. Don't be scared of death. There's more to come once you step through the curtain."

SEVEN

She must have fallen asleep. That was the only explanation for how difficult it was to open her eyes.

"Macey?" A hand followed her name, stroking along her brow.

Everything came flooding back. Where she was. What she'd done. Who she'd lost.

Sitting bolt upright, her gaze flickered around the room, trying to take in who was with her.

"Flint." Relief filled her as she saw her wraith sitting by the bed. It had been his hand on her forehead then. She was relieved he was okay.

"Hey, how are you feeling?" he asked softly.

"Achey," she answered. Her whole body felt heavy and exhausted, like she couldn't deal with even moving to react to the world around her.

"I'm not surprised. You did a lot of magic yesterday."

"I slept for that long?"

"Most of the day," Flint answered. "The others should be back soon."

"Are they alright?" She worried the sheet between her hands, trying not to be too concerned with the fate of her other men. They knew how to take care of themselves.

But Jared hadn't been in great shape when she'd left. And they were with Luc, who she wouldn't have trusted if she'd been paid to do so. There was something about the daimon she really couldn't bring herself to like very much.

"Cam says they're all fine. A bit battered and bruised, but nothing to be worried about."

"Hmm."

"They'll be back in an hour or two, you'll be able to see for yourself then."

"An hour or two? Why is it taking them so long?" she demanded, though her words were still coming out weak and hoarse.

"They didn't have access to the Staran where they were so they're..."

"But I used the Staran to get here," she interrupted.

"You did?"

"Yes. The lampads directed me to it."

"Ah. Yes, well I don't think the lampads would have let more people visit them. They're notorious for being antisocial."

"Believe it or not, I got that impression," she muttered, bitterness colouring every word.

"What did they show you, Macey?" he asked softly.

"It doesn't matter." She looked away, not wanting him to see the guilt she was sure rested in her eyes.

"Clearly it does." He reached forward and pulled her hand away from the sheet, slipping it into his and squeezing gently. "Tell me?" he pleaded.

Indecision warred within her. She longed to talk to someone about what had happened, even if it was only so she could move past it. Yet there was a part of her that loathed to admit how weak she'd been. It might just have been words the lampads tortured her with, but that didn't mean they hadn't hurt. Nor did it mean she hadn't taken them to heart. Her rampage the day before had been proof of that.

Guilt welled up inside her. Had she truly believed Amber would do that to her? Sweet, reliable Amber who'd been her friend even when she thought Macey was going to kill her.

A choking sound, across between a laugh and a sob escaped from Macey. After all this time, Amber's dream about Macey killing her had almost come true.

How could she have done that?

How could she have been so careless?

"Macey, please stop?" Flint begged. "Don't do this to yourself."

"But I..."

"No, Macey. You didn't. You were just being tested. It was all part of it..."

"I..." She stopped speaking as soon as she'd started. She didn't actually know what she wanted to say. A part of her wanted to apologise to her friends, but another part didn't want to face what had happened yet.

"Amber is waiting outside, Macey. She's worried about you. Not scared of you. Not hating you. She loves you like a sister and is here for you."

"But not Izban?" Her voice cracked as she asked.

An uneasy look flitted across Flint's face. "No, not Izban. It'll take him a little while to come around I think."

Cold dread flowed through her. All she kept doing was pushing the Ice Warden away with threats. If she wasn't careful, he really would end up betraying them. She had no idea how it would come about, or how he'd be able to do that to Amber, but something deep in gut told her this was a turning point and she needed to be careful.

"I know you're scared, Macey. I know your guilt and your shame don't want you to face her, but maybe talking to Amber is the best thing you can do."

She nodded slowly. "Maybe."

"I'll send her in." He got to his feet and leaned in to kiss her on the forehead.

Macey closed her eyes, enjoying the comfort he conveyed in his kiss. She longed to grab his arm and demand he stay with her, but she knew that was her nerves talking and not any genuine sentiment.

"I won't be far, just outside the door," he assured her, as if knowing what she was thinking.

"Thank you," she said weakly.

"You're welcome." He let go of her and strode over to the door. He stepped outside and she heard the murmur of voices, no doubt him talking to Amber and persuading her it was safe for her to come in.

The red-head slipped through the door moments later, hurriedly making her way over to the chair next to the bed and dropping down into it.

"How are you feeling?" she asked, compassion filling every word.

"Fine," she lied.

Amber's face said it all. There was no fooling the beithir.

"What happened?"

Macey considered for a couple of moments, wondering what she could tell Amber and what she needed to leave out. Before she'd even finished considering it, everything came tumbling out. Everything from the lampads test and the journey to get there. Everything that had gone through Macey's head once she'd returned to Malan's house.

She couldn't stop the words, but she did watch Amber's face, trying to work out how the other woman was taking it. Particularly the parts which painted Amber herself in a bad light.

"I know you wouldn't..."

"It doesn't matter," Amber interrupted softly. "I understand. It wasn't about me, our friendship, or even how much you trust me. You were in a vulnerable position and they latched on to every doubt you've ever had. I don't think any of us would have reacted any differently in your position. And anyone who says they would is lying."

"You really think that?" Macey asked. She hoped the other woman was telling the truth, but dared not assume. She didn't want to lose her friend, but nor did she want people to lie to her through fear.

"Yes, I really think that. It's not your fault, Macey. You should ignore anyone who says it is."

The way she phrased that made one thing clear in Macey's mind. Izban blamed her. And it was going to take more than an apology to bring him around.

"What should I do about Izban?" Macey asked carefully. "I know he must feel left out sometimes, with you being my friend and the other men being my partners. I don't want him to be a seventh wheel on this cart we're steering into danger."

Amber sighed. "I don't think Iz has ever been particularly social. Don't take it personally. He's got the social skills of a caveman and the empathy of a troll. And yes, I love him nonetheless." She blushed. "He's good at other things." She winked at Macey and just like that, the tension in the room ebbed away.

"By the way," Amber blushed even more, "I've been wondering how you do it. Four guys, it can't be easy."

Macey laughed, surprising herself. "Do you mean emotionally? Or physically?"

Amber grinned. "The latter. Not that I'm not interested in the relationship you have, but right now I'm feeling more like I want to know all the juicy details."

She wiggled an eyebrow suggestively at that last bit.

"Amber," Macey groaned. "Please don't use words like that."

"No? What about moist? There must be a lot of moisture when you all come together. You know, you being a water being and all that."

Macey's face was flaming red by now. "Can we go back to discussing the end of the world? That's so much less embarrassing than my love life."

Amber chuckled. "Well, let me tell you, using

magic during sex is amazing. Izban has this trick where he conjures ice while he-"

"Amber!"

The beithir laughed loudly. "Okay, okay, but what's really fun is when the ice starts to melt and-"

Macey threw a pillow at her friend, hitting her straight on the nose. She gasped and threw it back. Macey just about managed to evade it, but that meant the pillow hitting the lamp on the bedside table. It fell to the floor, the porcelain base shattering.

Before she could even move to pick up the shards, the door sprang open, Flint running into the room. Sparks covered his hands and he looked ready to interfere whatever cat fight the two women were involved in. They both looked at him as if they were surprised by his presence. They both knew that he'd been standing outside, waiting just in case the girls were going to attack each other. There was a distinct possibility that Izban was somewhere nearby too.

Amber pulled Macey off the bed, smiling innocently at Flint.

"We were just about to see if there's food somewhere. Macey is starving."

Yes, she was actually, now that she came to think of it. Food hadn't been a high priority but now that Flint was healed, the other guys on the way back and

Amber not dead by Macey's hands, she could really do with a meal.

"Waffles?" she asked hopefully.

Flint shook his head. "All we have is soup. Malan made it, so I don't know how good it is. The storm kelpies brought some fish earlier, but you're a vegetarian, so I didn't reserve any of that for you."

"How did Malan make soup?" Macey inquired. "He doesn't exactly have a body."

Flint shrugged. "No idea, I wasn't there to witness it. Maybe someone else made it and he's just claiming the credit for it. Who knows."

That sounded like something Malan would do. She just wished he'd made waffles instead of soup. She needed some sugar to keep her going and dispel all the dark memories still lingering at the corners of her mind.

"Let's have some food," she said, slightly more cheery than she thought.

BY THE TIME they'd finished their meal, Cam and the others arrived. All three of them were exhausted, but Jared looked healthier than he had when Macey had last seen him.

"We took a little stopover at the hedonist village," he explained at seeing her quizzical look, before hugging her tight. The other two had run over to Flint, checking on him, but Jared stayed with Macey, embracing her.

"Thanks for saving me," he whispered. "Somehow, you managed to save two Wardens in one day. I don't know how you do it, but thanks."

Macey smiled and pushed him just about far enough away so she could look him in the eyes.

"If I hadn't dragged you down in the water, you wouldn't have needed saving."

Instead of replying, he kissed her, his lips full of warmth and passion. The familiar incubus heat tingled on her skin. She peeked at his wrists. He was no longer wearing the cuffs. Good. She'd hated seeing him shackled like that. She couldn't imagine being cut off from her magic like that... well, actually, she could. The Mahoun had done something similar to her.

She returned his kiss, but her mind kept spinning. Now that everyone had returned and Flint had his powers back, they were going to have to go in search of the Mahoun, and defeat him.

Which sounded straight forward, but she knew it wouldn't be as easy as that. Nothing had been easy since the moment her brothers had been captured.

Her brothers.

Guilt welled up within her. Even more than when she'd thought her Wardens were in danger. So much had been going on that she hadn't given them a second thought.

On reflection, neither had her father when they'd visited him, which was odd, to say the least.

"Get me the kelpies," she instructed, not caring who actually followed her directions, so long as someone did.

It was time she had a talk with her own people.

She didn't recognise any of the men or women her father had sent with her, but that wasn't surprising. She'd been a classic sheltered Princess while living underwater. Just thinking about it had anger rising within her. There'd been no reason to keep her away from everyone. No other kelpie Princess in history had been treated that way. Unless it was something to do with her parentage.

Whatever the reason, she planned on getting to the bottom of it now.

"Princess."

"Your Highness."

"Your Majesty."

Each of the kelpies had their own way of formally greeting her, none of which were by her name. She wished she'd said yes to one of her men being in here with her, then at least she'd have someone who saw her as a person and not something to be worshiped.

"Please sit." She indicated towards the sofa opposite and all three of the kelpies sat hastily.

She smiled at them, but it did nothing to alleviate the nerves they were evidently feeling.

"You called for us?"

Macey held back a sigh of relief. At least one of them was talking to her and not in some falsely awestruck state.

"I did. What we discuss can't leave this room," she warned. It wasn't that she didn't want her allies to know, it was more about protecting her own reputation. Whether she liked it or not, she was the leader of their army. Even if she had no idea what that entailed.

"Of course," the boldest one answered. "We would never betray you."

She refrained from commenting, but the phrase never-say-never reverberated around her head. Particularly after what she had to ask them.

"I have a few questions about my brothers..." She studied each of their faces, trying to work out how they'd react.

"The Princes?" The middle kelpie frowned as she asked. "What about them? They were fine when we left the Loch."

"When you...left?" Macey's eyes widened. She couldn't be hearing that right.

"Yes, last week when you came to get us. Has something happened to the Princes since then?" The kelpie cocked her head to the side. Macey wasn't fooled. The woman really was worried. She wondered if there was anything in that.

"And you talked to my brothers?"

"Yes, all the time. I was one of Bruce's partners." The kelpie to her right shot her a look. "His sparring partners," she added hastily, but there was something about her words that suggested more to Macey.

"And you talked to him last week?"

"Yes, we were say...making arrangements for while I was away," the female kelpie answered.

"Did you know him before we went on land?" She crossed her fingers, hoping the woman would say yes.

"Of course, we're the same age."

Macey took the woman's word for it. She had no way of knowing if she was telling the truth or not. She certainly didn't recognise the other kelpie, but that didn't mean anything.

"Was he acting...strangely at all?"

"No. He was the same Bruce as when we were children."

Macey leaned back, not too sure what to make of it all. "When did he return to the Loch?"

"Just after you became a Warden, I think? The

two of them brought news of what had happened to you." The woman shrugged like it wasn't important.

Macey was lost for words. How had her brothers even known about her becoming a Warden? She hadn't seen them since she'd been taken by her men.

"Did they tell you how they knew that?" she asked slowly, almost dreading the answer.

"They said a Voice told them?" the kelpie on the right answered. He was older than the rest of them, which had Macey a little on edge. It felt wrong to be ranked higher than him.

"A Voice?" Her eyebrows creased together as the implications of that fell into place.

"Yes. I was skeptical at first too, but then Nessie confirmed what they were saying as true."

"Nessie?" Macey's voice took on a far away edge that she hated.

"Yes, your Aunt." The kelpie looked confused.

"What do you know of her?" Macey asked, choosing not to explain anything.

"The same as everyone. She was an adventurer when she was younger. That your Uncle wasn't enough for her, but he was okay with that. There are rumours she even had a fling with a human at one point."

Macey nodded, but didn't confirm or deny that. She knew the truth. Or at least, the supposed truth, but didn't want to admit to others that she could be proof of that.

"Anything else?"

"There are rumours she had secret children," the left kelpie answered as the woman next to him nodded.

"Rumours?"

That wouldn't be good. It could undermine everything Macey's father had worked for.

"Yes, but there's never been any proof. She's a formidable woman. A lot of people used to say she could take the crown if she wanted. Any children of hers would have been..."

"It's idle speculation," the older kelpie cut in. "And there is nothing to prove any of it. The rumours are twenty years old now, if Nessie had a child, they'd have shown themselves by now. And if she'd had more than one, then we'd already be at war."

The final word spun around Macey's mind. What the man didn't seem to have realised was that they were at war, just not within their kelpie community. This was one which could have a much bigger impact than just their Loch though. She kept the revelation to herself.

"Has my father announced which of my brothers is his heir yet?" She looked between the three kelpies, wondering which of them would break first. She wouldn't like to call it, they'd all seemed fairly forth-coming so far.

"Of course not, Your Highness," the woman answered softly. "How could he announce one of them his heir when you're here leading an army."

"That's not what I was..."

"Everyone is aware it's not your goal to use this to become Queen, but everyone is also aware that it takes a certain kind of person to lead troops. That's the kind of leader all of us want," the older kelpie answered. "That's the kind of kelpie I want to follow. Which is why I'm here."

"But..."

"Your father hasn't said anything yet," the younger man added. "I think he doesn't dare to. Announcing you're the heir would cause discord with anyone supporting your brothers' causes. But appointing one of them as his heir...it would cause havoc with anyone who respects the old ways. The strongest kelpie rules. That's how it has always been and how many of us want it to continue."

"And if I don't want to rule?" Her voice shook. Being Queen of the kelpies wasn't in her plan. She just wanted to defeat the Mahoun and live a peaceful life with her men.

"Then you'll be a better ruler than most," the older kelpie answered with finality.

MACEY ALMOST RAN out of the house, her mind swirling with all she'd just heard. It was going to take some time to make sense. Right now, it was going to distract her from battle, so she shoved it all in a far away corner of her mind, willing it to stay there. She didn't have time to think about civil war, her becoming Queen or why the fricking waves her brothers were back in the Loch. That didn't make any sense in the slightest. Either the kelpies were lying, or something else was going on. Maybe they weren't real? Or maybe they were being manipulated, mind-controlled? Who knew what the Mahoun was capable of.

"Everything alright?" Jared asked, walking towards her. The guys were standing a little apart from their other allies, all of them looking at her. Now that Flint had his powers back and they'd all returned from London, there was nothing that should be able to stop them from going into battle.

Macey really wanted a hug, but with everyone watching, she decided it would be better to simply take Jared's hand and give it a big squeeze.

"Not really," she muttered under her breath so that only he could hear. "It's all one big mess in the kelpie world, but I can't let this influence me just now. We need to make plans. What did Amber and Izban discuss with our allies while we were gone?"

Jared shrugged. "Better ask them yourself. It's not as if Izban would talk to us, and Amber's been busy... doing things with him. It's been a very enjoyable dessert."

He winked at Macey and heat flooded her belly. The incubus was insatiable, but she guessed that after he'd almost died, he was allowed to eat as much as he could, even if it was sexual energy siphoned off some of her friends.

They walked over to the others. The three kelpies were following them in the distance and Macey waited until they were close enough to hear her.

She took a deep breath and lifted her voice. "You have all come to fight at our side," she began, speaking as loud as she could. Something stirred within her and a tingle of magic ran over her skin. Air, she assumed. Maybe Air helped her increase her voice's strength.

"We would not have asked for this unless it was absolutely necessary. I believe you've all been told what we're up against. This isn't a mortal enemy, nor one any of you will have faced before. This isn't going to be easy. We don't know how best to defeat him."

"A little more upbeat," Jared whispered and squeezed her hand in reassurance.

Yes, she was getting to that.

"But we have defeated one of his kind before. We now know more about him and his kind than we did back then, so our chances are much higher. Last time, it was just as Wardens, but now, we have all of you fighting by our side. Together, we can defeat this evil before it spreads through all of our worlds. Just because it isn't affecting you yet doesn't mean it won't soon. The Kabouters are already feeling the effect, as are the kludde. The latter can't be here with us today because their magic is out of control and they might do more harm than good. They're suffering, and it's on us to do something about it. Now, will you fight with us, the Seven Wardens, to bring the Mahoun to justice?"

She shouted that last sentence, hoping it would bring others to join in. Alas, silence greeted her words. Were they not going to support them? Had she messed up? Was her speech not convincing enough?

Finally, one of the kelpies roared, "Yes! We will stand with you, your Majesty!"

Oh no. Couldn't they just keep calling her Princess or Highness? Majesty was a step in the wrong direction, a very wrong one that could lead to civil war.

"We're with you!" a very short Kabouter shouted, his voice surprisingly deep for his size. Then, everybody joined in, calling out statements of support, some even stamping on the marshy ground for emphasis.

Macey smiled, relief flooding her. They weren't going to leave. They were going to fight. Now, the big question was, where were they going to take the fight?

"Macey?" Amber asked quietly, having appeared behind the kelpie. "Malan told us some stuff while you were away. It might help us, or it might not. You know how he is."

Macey sighed. "What did he say? And why can't he just tell us now?"

She looked around for the bodiless prophet, but couldn't see him anywhere.

"He's left," the beithir whispered. "Don't tell anyone, we don't want them to think he abandoned us. He said he had to go and find someone who could help us. He didn't tell us who, but he did tell us something else."

"Yes?" Macey asked impatiently.

"Activate the markings and you will find a doorway that will lead to doom or salvation," Amber recited. "That's exactly what he said. Do you think he means the tattoos on your back?"

Macey frowned. She couldn't think of any other markings that they'd come across recently. The ones on her skin were still a mystery. She knew they repre-sented the other Wardens, but she had no idea why she was carrying them. Maybe this was the answer. Question was, how was she supposed to activate them?

"Please tell me he gave you instructions to activate the markings?" she sighed, but Amber shook her head, suppressing a smile.

"Of course he didn't. I think he wasn't happy about telling us this much already. I guess it wasn't vague enough for him."

Macey laughed. "Yes, that sounds like Malan. I guess we have to trust him. So far, he's not led us in any wrong direction, although I can't say he's always led us in the right one, either."

"He's a weird man... being, that's for sure," Amber agreed. "Shall we ask the others if they have any idea about what to do with the markings? But maybe not here. I'll tell our allies we're making last minute preparations, you go inside with the others and figure something out."

Macey nodded and watched as the beithir confidently strode towards the Kabouters.

"MAYBE WE NEED TO HAVE SEX?" Jared suggested with a wolfish grin. "All of us?"

Izban growled. "No way. If you even suggest this again, I'm out."

"I do love a good orgy," the incubus muttered, but didn't press the issue further. They all knew that Izban was already at the outskirts of their group, and nobody wanted him to retreat completely.

"Maybe we need to give you some of our magic?" Cam proposed instead. "Somehow point it at our respective markings and see what happens?"

"I wouldn't want to burn her," Flint warned. "And I'm not sure lightning would be good for her either. No offense, Amber."

He smiled at the beithir who'd just entered the room.

"None taken. Macey has felt my magic before however. Maybe she just needs to think about it? Concentrate on it somehow?"

Macey shrugged. "I can try it. It sounds a little too easy though."

"Sometimes, not everything is as hard as it seems," Flint said in a voice that sounded a lot like Malan's. Cam elbowed him in the ribs.

"I better show you my tattoos while I do this," Macey suggested. "Tell me if anything changes."

She took off her bra, almost enjoying Izban's shocked gaze. She stepped towards the sofa and lay on it so that they could all see her back. She closed her eyes, hoping that would make it easier to focus. Not that she really knew what to focus on. She couldn't feel the tattoos, they didn't hurt or make themselves noticed in any other way. She sighed. This was going to be one of those annoying and seemingly unsolvable quests. All part of being a Warden. Bah.

Macey concentrated on her water magic. That one was going to be the easiest, so it made sense to start out with it. Problem was, she had no idea what to do. She didn't want to drench the room in water, or herself, or anyone. She created a few drops of water and let them fall on the bare skin of her back.

"There's water," Flint informed her. "But the marking isn't doing anything."

It would have been too easy. Instead of physically creating water, Macey thought of how the magic felt like. The cool, slippery, calming essence of the magic she'd wielded for years. Even just thinking about it relaxed her. Yes, the magic could be wild and destructive, but while it was slumbering within her, it was a peaceful loch that mirrored her thoughts and emotions. Unless she wasn't feeling peaceful, then it changed into something more violent. It happened. Now that she was looking at her magic, she felt it calling to her. She took a deep breath and jumped, diving into the loch, entering it with an elegant jump that would have made any Olympic athlete gasp. Or so she liked to think.

If this had been real water, she would have shifted into her kelpie form, but as she didn't really have a body in her mind - yes, it was very confusing - she stayed as she was, somehow being able to breathe without a problem.

She swam around a little, exploring the loch that had been within her forever but which she'd never dived into before. It had always seemed impenetrable and not as inviting as it had a moment ago when she'd taken the plunge.

"Something's happening!" she heard from far away. Good. That meant she was supposed to continue swimming, or exploring, or whatever had worked for the marks to activate. She let herself drift to the water's surface and rolled onto her back, looking up into the darkness that was her mind. Not because she was evil; no, it was a familiar, gentle darkness that felt soothing rather than threatening. She spread her arms and legs, floating, completely relaxed. She should do this more often. It felt really good.

"Your water mark is glowing!"

She smiled, until the same voice continued, "Move on to the next one!"

Macey sighed. She didn't want to leave this place. She'd not had a break in weeks, always hurrying from one place to another, never resting. Still, her sense of duty prevailed and with one last splash of water, she left her inner loch, focussing on another kind of magic that was similar: ice.

She thought of what she knew about ice. It was

cold, deadly, majestic. A silent killer. Strong. Able to break things. Avalanches, icicles, slippery ice on the ground. The images flashed through her mind and step by step, her skin became colder. She looked down at the loch beneath her, not at all surprised when she saw a thin sheet of ice covering its surface. Hopefully it wasn't permanent. She really didn't want to carry a piece of Izban within her. That was Amber's job.

NINE

S he looked in the mirror, trying to work out if anything was different about her. She'd managed all of the elements save one: Wind. Why it was Cam's mark that eluded her, she had no idea. Maybe it was all tied into the mists? They never had seemed all that friendly.

"Staring at yourself isn't going to help."

Macey shrieked and spun around, grabbing her shirt from the chair beside her and hastily throwing it back on.

"Lucien," she hissed. "What are you doing here?"

"Admiring the view." He lifted a suggestive eyebrow, but it was so at odds with the rest of his expression that she ignored it.

"And you thought just appearing in my room was the way to go?"

"I am your daimon," he pointed out. "Your Wardens did a good job at trying to lose me, I will admit. But they didn't take into account that I don't need to know where you are to be able to find you."

"That makes no sense," she snapped, concern filling her as she wondered about the implications.

"Doesn't it?"

"For a guide, you sure ask a lot of open questions."

"A guide's job isn't to tell their charge the answer, Macey. If I did that, then I might as well write an instruction manual."

"One would be appreciated," she muttered, trying not to taunt herself with how much easier that would make things.

"Whether that is the case or not, it's not something I can provide."

"Have you been talking to Malan?" She put her hands on her hips, more confident now she was covered. Even so, she hoped his eyes wouldn't stray to the messy bed and have him think those kinds of thoughts about her.

Luc laughed. "You have nothing to fear, your sex life doesn't bother me at the moment." He seemed nonchalant on the surface, but she could tell there was something else beneath the surface. She didn't know what though. The daimon was difficult for her to work out.

"Don't say that," she hissed.

"The word sex? You have four lovers at the moment, right?"

"Yes, sex."

"I didn't take you for a prude. How disappointing. I'd hoped you'd be more like the nymphs."

"What's that supposed to mean?" Anger flashed beneath the surface like a riptide under a calm sea. If the daimon wasn't careful, he was going to find himself well and truly drenched.

"How is the rage coming along, kelpie? Do you have it under control yet?"

"It was never out of my control," she snapped.

"The fields outside suggest differently."

"That was nothing more than an accident."

"I see, you're going to be one of those." He pulled out one of the chairs from beneath the simple wooden table. He flopped down on it, his dark wings flapping ever so slightly as he did.

"One of what?" She was curious, but didn't want to admit it quite yet. That would mean letting him win.

"Sit," he instructed.

She thought about arguing but decided it was too detrimental. Perhaps in his own round about way he'd tell her something useful. Or at least, more useful than Malan had. Not that it took much. Talking about something other than food made anyone more useful than the disembodied prophet.

Without waiting any longer, she perched herself on the end of the bed, only just refraining from kicking the loose bra she spotted underneath it so he wouldn't see.

"One of what?" she repeated.

"You know what, Macey. One of the ones who refuses to accept who they are or what they're meant to do. It's never their fault and they never know what to do. When I received you as my charge, I was actually excited. You seemed to have a certain level of acceptance which isn't often found in heroes..."

"I'm not a hero."

"Correction. You're not a hero, yet. But one day, they will sing songs about you and tell your story."

"I hope not," Macey said despite herself. She wasn't the type for that. Just like she wasn't the type to become Queen.

"Regardless of your feelings, you will be. But I was excited. A hero who finally accepted their fate. Who would do what was necessary without it being forced on them by the gods..."

"I thought you said the gods were dead?" she interrupted, receiving a scolding look in return.

"The gods are dead, but I'm talking about the past. Have you any idea how infuriating some of those Greek heroes were? The playwrights were correct in things either being a tragedy or a comedy. You should have seen Hercules." He shook his head and muttered something unintelligible.

"Hercules, son of Zeus?" she checked, suddenly glad she'd wasted a couple of days binge watching the cartoon royalty human children liked to watch.

"The one and only. His twelve trials? All performed by his daimon." Luc's eyes flared.

She still wasn't sure what he was actually getting at. Nor what he wanted from her. But the anger had ebbed away slightly, allowing her to think straight for a moment.

"I thought daimons only had one charge?" she asked slowly, recalling what Cam had said when they'd first encountered Luc.

He sighed. "We do. But we're reborn every time our charge is done. I've seen a lot of lives, but you're the only one I'm charged with in this one."

"Right." She leaned back against the wall, not sure what to do about the unknown man opposite her. He claimed to be there to help her, as her guide, but that didn't quite add up with the experience she was having. He certainly hadn't done much helping as far as she was concerned. "So...you're here to help me?"

"I can only help if you accept my aid."

"Fine, I accept it."

He laughed. "That's not how it works. You have to actually accept it within you, not just say the lie out loud."

He slunk his hand into the pocket of his coat and Macey flinched back for reasons unknown to her. Something about this man had her on edge and she didn't have the slightest clue what.

"Relax, I only want a drink." As if to illustrate his point, he removed a metal hip flask and popped the top off, taking a swig.

"May I?" she asked, her voice shaking. The past couple of days had been rough. A drink would certainly take the edge off.

"Sure." He held out the flask and she got up from her position on the bed to get it from him, only slightly resentful he was making her work for it.

She took the cold metal in her hand and brought the flask to her lips. Swallowing deeply, she glugged down the liquid inside. Or she tried to. Instead of it slipping down her throat as she'd expected, it caught in her throat and a loud cough rattled through her.

"What the fuck is that?" she demanded through the coughs.

"Fortified mead." The daimon shrugged.

"Mead isn't very Greek," she muttered.

"Neither is living beneath the Thames, but I did that too."

"You're very sarcastic for a guide."

"You're very infuriating for a hero."

"That's because I'm not one." Something bubbled up within her, reminding her of the rage of the day before. She tried to gain control again, not wanting to go through the same strain and terror again.

"Do you actually believe it when you say that?" he demanded.

"I don't know," she admitted sharply. Then sighed. "I'm sorry, it's been a rough..." she tried to count in her head but couldn't work it out. So much had happened that her days ran together a bit, especially with her time in the Voice's castle to take into account.

"No one said your path was going to be easy," he pointed out.

"No one gave me a choice," she spat, throwing the flask back at him.

Her efforts were somewhat ruined by the ease he caught it with.

"No one said you'd get that either."

"Are you purposefully so infuriating?" she demanded, her nostrils flaring and her hands tingling with the urge to use some kind of magic on him. At this rate, she couldn't even predict which of the six would come out of her. Though she'd had the most practice with water, fire had come just as easily yesterday. Burning Luc to a crisp did sound satisfying.

She flexed her fingers, unsure if she'd actually act on her thoughts or just think them.

"No. I'm telling you what you need to hear, Macey," he shot back, getting to his feet.

He boxed her in; his height should have been intimidating, but it just seemed to egg Macey's anger on that little bit more.

"I hate to disagree..." She lifted her hand but Luc was quicker, closing his hand around her wrist and squeezing gently.

"Just because you don't want to, doesn't mean you don't need to. Now I need to know, are you going to make my job more difficult than it is already?" His jovial tone had disappeared, leaving pure threat in his words.

Macey's eyes hardened as she looked up at him, only just noticing how perfectly proportioned his features were. It was as if the term sculpted by gods had been coined for him. Macey shook her head, breaking the tension between them. But not her rage. She could still feel that and not in a way she was used to. She wasn't simply frustrated. This was something more.

What if...no. She couldn't think that. There was no way she was housing one of Mahoun's siblings. That would be too obvious.

"No, I won't make it more difficult," she accepted, begrudging him every single word.

"Good. Now sit down and I'll tell you the rest." His calm and light air had returned along with a smile.

Macey shook her head. He made no sense.

"But first, show me your back."

"You've already seen it," she huffed, blushing at the earlier embarrassment.

"I need to see your marks properly or I won't be able to help you," he said, his patience amazing her. By now, she'd probably be screaming at herself rather than look as calm and collected as he did.

She sighed and turned her back to him, lifting her shirt.

"Beautiful," he muttered and she was very tempted to drop her top again. Hopefully, he was talking about the marks, not about her body. She really didn't want to have to deal with an admirer as well as an annoying daimon.

"They're glowing," he observed. "But one isn't."

"Wind," she nodded. "Somehow I couldn't connect to it."

"But you did manage to activate Air?"

Macey nodded, not wanting to expand on that. Air lived within her, so that had been one of the easiest elements. She was connected to Air, almost as closely as she was to her water magic.

"Air and Wind are very similar," the daimon said. "Maybe if you focus on Air again and then gently shift your focus, without letting go completely, it might work."

It was worth a try. She closed her eyes and thought of Air again. It was easier than it had been earlier. This time, she immediately felt the presence of its magic all around her. She was back hovering above her inner loch again, feeling the air's gentle embrace. She wasn't swaying, there was no wind, it was simply holding her in the air as if she was standing on solid ground. She trusted Air completely not to let her go.

She thought of Wind. That was far more unpredictable and violent. Wind could topple her and blow her down into the water. No, she didn't want that, she much preferred the gentleness of Air.

Well, there it was. She was afraid.

The realisation shocked her. How could she be afraid of one of her men's elements? She'd never been scared of Cam, and being scared of his magic was just weird. Wind was everywhere, it was refreshing when it got too hot, it helped boats sail, it transported seeds to new pastures. Wind was good, not just dangerous.

She tried to focus on all the positive things she knew about Wind. When she'd first met the guys, Cam had created mini tornados that had whirled around the palms of his hands. Even though they should have been threatening, she'd thought them incredibly cute. She smiled and focussed on that memory. Cam, his laugh, his enthusiasm for his magic.

Slowly, a breeze began to blow, gently kissing Macey's hair, but she didn't flinch away. She was still held by Air, and Wind was just another playmate, not a threat. They were going to be a fun pair to hang out with. Air, the steady one, Wind, the turbulent one.

She raised a hand and felt for the Wind. At first, nothing happened, just the same breeze tousling her hair, but then, something gripped her hand. She squeezed, her eyes not seeing anything but her magic feeling the new, strong power she was now holding. She was touching Wind, even though that was supposed to be impossible.

Suddenly, without any warning at all, she was thrown back into her body, looking at Luc in bewilderment.

"We need to go," he said urgently, grabbing his hand and pulling her out of the room.

She was far too shocked to resist, her mind still trapped halfway between her inner, peaceful loch and the harsh reality.

He led her out of Malan's house and into the fog where everyone was staring at a strange glistening cloud. It was about as big as a large van, bright blue, and pulsating in a steady beat, its colour increasing every time.

"What is that?" she gasped, her expression mimicking that of all the other onlookers: a mixture of wonder and fear.

"That's our path out of here," the daimon explained just as the other Wardens reached them. "You've opened the portal, now you have to step through it."

"It worked?" Cam asked in surprise. "I thought I felt something but wasn't sure what had happened."

"Yes, yes, she did amazingly, now shush, let her gather herself. She needs to be completely focussed to lead all of us through the portal."

Macey was having trouble following the conversation. Focusing? That seemed impossible. If only Luc hadn't brought her back from her out-of-body experience this suddenly. She'd be fine then, but now, she was confused. Everything was happening so quickly.

Hands grabbed her shoulders and squeezed until she looked up, right into the daimon's fiery eyes.

"You're the only one who can lead us through that portal, Macey," he said, his voice serious. "You need to concentrate on your destination as hard as you can."

"But we don't know our destination," she protested. "I have no idea where the Mahoun is."

"You remember his castle?" he asked and she nodded, wondering how he even knew about that.

"Think of that. Remember as many details as you can. It's not the exact place that's important, it's the essence of his home. Think of the Mahoun, think of his castle, think of all the evil you'll be able to prevent by defeating him. Can you do that?"

His expression had changed to something almost desperate. She wondered how many of his charges had failed in the past. How many he'd lost during impossible quests.

She grit her teeth and nodded.

"Okay, I'll do that. Will you all follow or how does this work?"

Luc smiled at her, his entire face lighting up.

"Good girl. Yes, we'll be right behind you. Once you've arrived, keep your focus until everyone is through, or the portal will collapse. Remember, you're the one controlling it."

"Why is she suddenly so special?" Izban muttered in the background, but Macey ignored him. There were more important things to think about.

She looked around at her allies. Kelpies, kabouters, her fellow Wardens, and in the distance, she knew that the na fir ghorma were waiting as well, ready to help if needed. It wasn't a massive army, but it was better than just the eight of them. Seven, if she didn't count Air, which nobody ever seemed to do.

"Are you ready?" she shouted, hoping everyone would hear her.

A resounding 'yes' echoed back to her. Good. They were still feeling the effect of her earlier speech. No need to make another.

"Follow me!"

She took a deep breath and stepped towards the pulsing blue cloud.

"Do I just walk into it?" she whispered to Luc.

"I believe so."

That made her turn around and stare at the daimon.

"You *believe* so? Does that mean you don't actually know?"

He shrugged. "It seems like the only option. We'll find out if it works soon enough."

She huffed, repressing a string of curses. This man was even more infuriating than Malan.

Ignoring him, she looked at the other Wardens and Rónàn. All six of them were assembled behind her, their eyes hardened, their bodies tense. They were ready for battle, just like she was.

"Let's do this," she said, and focussed on her memories of being held by the Mahoun. Usually, she tried to avoid even thinking of her imprisonment, but now, she let them all flow back into her, her mind filling with the memories of darkness and fear. The screams in the distance. The absence of her magic. The moment Amber attacked her. The strange visions the Mahoun had shown her.

She took another deep breath and stepped into the cloud.

TEN

When she stepped into the cloud, time froze. As did her heart. She couldn't breathe, the pressure on her chest was too much. She tried to walk, but she was trapped, suspended in the air, the weird cloud pressing against her from all sides.

Despite the pain, she concentrated once again, focussing on the Mahoun and his dark castle. She closed her eyes so the swirling blue all around her wouldn't distract her. it was already hard to think with all the sound of sizzling electricity. This cloud wasn't like anything she'd ever seen. Not that it was a cloud, she was fairly certain about that.

Focus.

The Mahoun. His Voice. Amber. The men dragging her out into the courtyard. Flying away on the beithir. Realising it was all just a game the Mahoun was playing with their minds. Their actual escape.

The pressure around her chest lessened the more she thought of who she wanted to find.

The dungeon. The cold. The dark. The fear. The loneliness. Thoughts of never again being with her men.

Suddenly, the cloud flared so bright she could see it through her closed eyelids, then it spit Macey out. She stumbled onto hard stone ground, just about managing to stay upright.

Remembering the daimon's words, she kept her mind fixed on her memories, hoping they'd be enough to get everyone else through.

Cam was the first to step through the cloud, followed by Amber and Izban. Little lightning bolts were swirling all around the mage's body, probably a side effect of the electricity within the portal.

When the other Wardens arrived, Macey's concentration began to waver. It was getting more and more difficult to remember the things she'd tried so hard to forget. The ache in her chest when her magic had been blocked. The fear for her men, not knowing where they were. The fear of dying. The disappointment and frustration when all her visions of freedom turned out to be false.

"You can do this," Amber said, suddenly in front

of Macey, gently touching her shoulders. "Think of how long I was there. Think of what I must have felt."

Macey really didn't want to do that, but she knew she had to. Her own memories weren't enough.

She sighed and put herself in Amber's shoes. Weeks of being imprisoned. Missing Izban. Realising she was in love with him and being ripped away from him that very moment. All the hallucinations showing a kelpie attacking her. The hunger pains ripping through her stomach.

She shuddered as her imagination took on a life of its own. Amber had told her a few of the things that had happened to her, but not all. Some of the things she was now picturing in her mind had likely never happened, but they helped keep up the portal.

"Almost there, hold on!" Flint shouted, helping a kelpie who'd fallen to the ground after stepping from the cloud.

It took another few minutes before everyone was through. Luc was the final one to step through the portal.

"You can let go now," he said gently and with a sigh of relief, Macey pushed away all the dark thoughts and memories, taking in her surroundings for the first time.

They were in a bland, barren landscape filled with

nothing but dirt and muddy ground. Right now, they were standing on a stone plateau that was looking over the wastes all around them. There was no castle in sight.

"Are you sure this is the right place?" Amber asked hesitantly. "This doesn't look like someone lives here."

Luc clucked his tongue in disapproval. "Ask the incubus, he knows."

They all turned to Jared, whose eyes had taken on a dreamy sheen.

"Illusion," he said between clenched teeth as if it was hard to speak. "Give me a moment and I'll try and remove it."

Macey put a hand on his arm, sending him a burst of energy. She had no idea how she was doing it, but now that she'd activated all the marks on her back, she felt a strange affinity with his magic. Not just his, all of theirs. She doubted she'd ever be as good at Earth magic as Jared was, but she was convinced she could at least control it in a basic way.

She looked towards the direction Jared was staring at. The air above the arid ground was quivering slightly, as if there was great heat just below it. Slowly, very slowly, she began to see what he was seeing. There was a castle indeed, a large, massive structure built right in front of them. It maybe a mile away, no more, but yet it had been hidden from view until now. They could have probably walked up right to its gates without ever knowing it was there. Luckily, they had Jared with them, an incubus versed in all sorts of illusions.

"Is that where you were held?" Izban asked his girlfriend, wrapping an arm around her shoulders in a protective gesture.

Amber nodded. "Yes. I never thought I'd come back here, at least not voluntarily. Let's hope he's not expecting us." She shuddered and Macey felt the same shiver running over her body. It all felt real now. They were going to have to fight the Mahoun and it wasn't sure if any of them would survive.

Was it worth it? She thought of the Kludde, plagued by their own magic; the Kabouters, threatened by earthquakes; the sidhe, twisted in some way or another. And of course the Staran, still not safe from being manipulated by the Mahoun or one of his siblings.

Yes, it was worth it. The world needed to be rid of his evil.

Some of the people around her were rubbing their eyes, only now realising that the illusion had been lifted.

"By the waves," one of the kelpies muttered, her mouth hanging open. "How did that get here?"

"It was here all along," Jared said with a shrug. "I just helped you see it."

"Are you ready to be a hero?" Luc whispered into Macey's ear, suddenly being a lot closer to her than she'd remembered.

"No," she whispered back.

"Good. Overconfidence wouldn't be good in this case. But trust me, you'll do well. Now lead these people into battle before the alarm is raised and the castle's defences are activated."

She nodded tensely, looking at the castle one last time before turning to her allies.

"It's time," she said loudly. "Kabouters, as discussed, Jared will lead you through the earth and you'll enter the castle that way. Kelpies, you're with me. Amber, you'll fly in together with Izban, who'll try and hide you both. If you manage to get inside, you open the gates for us. Luc..."

She faltered, unsure what the daimon's role was going to be. Amber had filled her in on the plan earlier, so even though she was now telling everyone what to do, it hadn't actually been her brainchild.

"I'll be with you," Luc said calmly. "I'm going to watch your back.

Macey nodded, strangely glad that the daimon was going to be around. As arrogant and unhelpful as he was, he still seemed powerful enough to be a good ally.

Jared led his group of Kabouters to one side and began to talk with their leaders, while Amber and Izban walked away to the other side, embracing. They were preparing not to see each other again, Macey realised. Maybe she should say goodbye to her men as well, but that felt like she was being defeatist. No, she was going to assume that everyone was going to live by the end of this. Nobody was going to die. She wouldn't allow it.

"We can do this," Rónàn said from behind her, echoing her thoughts.

She turned and smiled at him. "Yes, we can."

Before she could turn away again, he bent down and pressed his lips against hers, a kiss far too quick to be more than a promise of more.

"We're ready!" Jared called out.

"As are we," Izban said gravely, his arm still holding Amber close.

"Then let's do this!" Macey shouted. "Whoever kills the Mahoun is the champion!"

It was supposed to be a bit of a joke, something to lighten the mood, but the others started to pick up her chant.

"The champion! The champion!"

Oh no, she'd created a monster.

~

NO ONE HAD EVER WARNED her that war was so boring. In all the history books, it was so glorious and full of action. This...not so much. The first assault on the castle had led to precisely nothing. There was some kind of force field around the castle which had rebuffed the Kabouters underground and Amber and Izban above it.

"Please tell me one of you know what we're up against?" she begged the people surrounding her.

They shook their heads, all in various states of denial about the situation.

"Luc?" She turned to the daimon, hoping he'd have some kind of answer. He was supposed to be her guide, yet he wasn't doing much guiding right at that moment.

"I'm sorry, this isn't anything I've ever come across before," he admitted.

Macey kicked the ground, stubbing her toe. She scowled, unsure about what she was meant to be doing anymore. How was she supposed to defeat Mahoun and his siblings if she was flummoxed while trying to break into a castle.

The air buffeted against them as Amber landed, shifting back into her human form almost instantly. Izban rushed forward and threw a blanket around her, covering her nakedness.

Macey just about refrained from rolling her eyes. She knew Amber wasn't shy about her body. She was a shifter, it was born into her not to be. If Izban hadn't been so frustrating, the gesture might even have been cute but now she wasn't so sure. She'd seen the way he watched the others. He needed to be watched and she wasn't sure who she'd be able to set on him.

One of the kelpies, maybe? No. It couldn't be one of them. He'd be able to freeze their water magic too easily. Which also took out anyone who could control fire. Ice would melt under heat, true, but it would also put the flames out. One of the other Wardens then? Amber was out for the obvious reasons, but the others?

She glanced between them, trying to work out who to trust with this. She loved and trusted all her men but she was sure not all of them fully supported her mistrust of Izban. Her eyes settled on the daimon. He hadn't known Izban long enough yet. Mistrust would be in his nature.

"Luc, a word." She indicated to the side with her head, making it clear she expected him to obey without question.

The daimon gave her a lazy smile, as if knowing exactly what she was thinking. She ignored him. It wasn't worth explaining things to him at this point. Not with all the ears listening.

"What can I do for you?" he asked once they were far enough away from the others.

"What do you think about Izban?" She fell into step beside him as he headed towards the hill looking over the Keep. Even if this discussion was a bust, she'd be able to get a good view of where they were trying to attack. Macey didn't know enough about warfare to know whether it would actually help or not, but anything which gave them an advantage at the moment was a welcome change.

"The Ice Warden?"

"Yes."

"Cold."

"Very funny." She gave him a look that contradicted her words.

"I don't know him well enough to have an opinion," Luc answered.

"You must have some ideas," she counted.

"Of course. I'm your guide, I've been watching for longer than you think."

"So?"

She waited for him to answer as they continued to walk in silence. The hill was getting steeper and she could feel the burn in her legs but chose to ignore it.

"I think you're looking for trouble in the wrong place," he said evenly.

"But?"

"But not everyone is going to be what they seem."

"Cryptic," she muttered, already feeling more annoyed than she should. It wasn't fair for her to have such high expectations on him. The only person she had the right to expect things from was herself.

"But yes, I'll watch him for you."

"How did you-"

"You're very easy to read, Macey. Your mistrust is written all over your face. Much like your anger is on occasion too. You might want to watch it around the beithir too. She's your friend, true, but you can't ask her to choose between you and the man she loves."

The words sunk in slowly. Mostly because she wasn't ready to accept them yet.

"So what do I do?" she whispered.

"I can't answer that. You're the only one who can. But you need to trust the other Wardens. Any weaknesses in the bonds you share will only play into the enemies hands."

"What did you just say?" Macey asked eagerly, an idea forming in her head.

"Any weaknesses will be an advantage to your enemies?" He cocked his head, a puzzled expression on his face.

She didn't explain to him. She couldn't. The less he knew about this the better. In fact, there was only one person she'd be able to talk to about the plan forming in her head and she doubted he'd like it. Still, he was a Warden. He'd do his duty, as they all would.

"You look like you're plotting something."

"Oh I am, you gave me a great idea." She went up

on her tiptoes and kissed his cheek, leaving him shocked in her wake.

For the first time in a while, she felt like she had a handle on the situation. And more importantly, a plan in place. All she had to do now was hope Izban played his role.

ELEVEN

"Why are you looking so smug?" Jared demanded between bites of his breakfast. "We haven't gotten any closer to breaking the castle's defences and you wouldn't let us do anything fun last night."

"Too right I didn't," she replied, carefully avoiding his real question. "There are far too many people about for us to do that." And she didn't want her night time activities reported back to the kelpies. It was one thing them knowing she had four men, quite another for them to do it and get caught.

And then there was Luc...

Her gaze strayed to the daimon, who was busy chatting with Cam, no doubt about some mystical and ancient being the rest of them hadn't heard of. So long as she was told about whatever beast it was before she had to face it in the flesh. Though that was seeming less and less likely as time went on. There was certainly more to this world than she first thought.

"Macey? You didn't answer the question."

She ignored him, her attention already on a frazzled looking Amber barging out of her tent.

Right on schedule.

"Izban?" she called. At first, it almost seemed like she was just calling for him. But Macey could hear the concern in her voice.

At least that meant the Ice Warden had done what she'd expected him too. Guilt welled up inside her at the thought of hiding this from the others, but she knew she had to. For this to work, they couldn't know.

"Have any of you seen Izban?" Amber asked, reaching the fire around which they sat.

"Was he not with you?" Cam asked, breaking in his conversation.

Amber shook her head violently. "No. His spot in our tent is cold too. He hasn't been there in a good while," she said before anyone could ask her how long he'd been gone.

"When did you last see him?" Rónàn asked, ushering her to one of the log seats and handing her a steaming cup of tea.

She took it reluctantly, but Macey could tell she

wanted the support of her friends. Her heart broke a little for the beithir, this next day or so wasn't going to be easy for her. Not in the slightest. And if this went wrong...

It didn't bear thinking about.

"Was he alright last night?" Rónàn continued with the questions.

"He seemed to be, yes. Perfectly normal. He kissed me goodnight and then we..." She scuffed the dirt with her shoe, a blush spreading across her cheeks.

Beside Macey, Jared nodded, confirming she was saying exactly what Macey thought she was.

"And then he was just gone?" Rónàn's face pulled into a frown, as if he just couldn't work it out.

Macey stayed silent, not wanting to reveal what she knew. Now wasn't the time, even if it hurt her friend in the short term. Amber would understand it was for the good of them all. And the world.

She looked up at precisely the wrong time, catching Luc's eyes. The daimon gave her a knowing look, like he'd seen what she was up to and worked the rest out. The implications of that were ever so slightly terrifying, but she didn't break.

"We'll find him," Rónàn assured the beithir. "He has to be in the camp still, there's nowhere else to go."

"If only that were true," Amber muttered, giving a haunted glance at the Keep behind them.

Macey didn't turn to look. She didn't want to face the place she'd been held captive until she had to. Maybe that was the coward's way of dealing with things but at this point she didn't care. She'd rather be a coward than a quivering mess and that's what the castle would leave her as, she was sure of it.

"He can't be there," Jared butt in. "If he is then he'd have found what we've all failed to so far."

"Maybe he did. Maybe he called his aos si and found a way..." Amber's eyes grew large, as if becoming convinced that was true.

"He tried that already," Cam pointed out. "I doubt it would work any better the second time."

They all nodded and relief flooded Amber's face as a result. She was so worried for him, which only tore Macey up inside. She didn't want to be doing this to her friend but it truly was safer if she didn't know the truth.

"I'm sorry, I know we don't have time for this. Just give me a little longer and I'll be ready for the day." Amber's face changed suddenly, growing from drawn and worried to determined. This time it was admiration which flooded through Macey. Her friend was truly a very special woman. Her bravery and determination were something to be admired.

"What's the plan for today?" Luc asked, looking around the circle.

"We need to prepare for another attack on the Keep," Macey answered, speaking up for the first time since Amber had joined them. "But not attack until dusk."

Seven heads swivelled in her direction, each of them looking at her with differing levels of disbelief.

"Why dusk?" Flint asked the question they were probably all thinking.

"A feeling," Macey lied. In truth, she was hoping to have had a signal by then and wanted to be sure they didn't waste the opportunity they now had. If they wasted it, there was a chance the woman who was fast becoming her best friend would never speak to her again. Even thinking that didn't sit well with Macey. Just as she didn't want to lose her men, she didn't want to lose her friend either.

"You want us to stake our lives on a feeling?" Cam asked, raising an eyebrow in slight disbelief.

"Why not a feeling? Hasn't our whole relationship been based on a gut feeling?"

She watched as Cam spluttered but didn't confirm or deny it. She didn't need him to. She knew as well as he did that he'd taken her to the house because it felt like the right thing to do. She almost laughed. That seemed like so long ago. A completely different time when she really was nothing more than a kelpie princess kidnapped by two wraiths and an incubus.

She sighed. It was true it had been simpler then but she couldn't bring herself to regret the rest of their journey. It had brought her to so many different places and met so many different people. Without it, she wouldn't have found Rónàn. Or Amber. Or Luc. People made this whole thing worth it.

"Okay then," Rónàn said slowly. "What are we going to do until dusk?"

"I could think of a few things," Jared muttered and while Macey was tempted to give in to his desires, she knew there were more important things to do.

"I need to train. The markings are itching and I think I need to see if I can access their magic." She'd been tempted to scratch her back the entire night. Something was happening to the tattoos and while it didn't feel like something bad or threatening, she needed to explore her newfound connection to the other elements. Also, this training would give Izban more time, something he likely needed.

"Amber, do you want to join me? I think lightning will be the hardest element to work with."

The beithir nodded, still a little pale from worry. Macey was going to have to distract her as much as she could. She didn't want her friend to suffer. Although if this went wrong, she might no longer have a friend, but an enemy. She sighed inwardly. Was it worth that? Losing their friendship? She thought of all the pain Amber had gone through at the hands of the Mahoun and decided that it was. As long as the Mahoun was put to justice, it would be worth it. If it all failed though... she didn't want to think about that. It had to work. It just had to.

"Yes, I'll help you," Amber said softly, her usual smile gone.

"Call us if you need any of us as well," Cam offered, nodding at the other Wardens. "Guess we'll do some training ourselves."

Macey took Amber outside, a short distance away from their camp, far enough that they weren't watched by curious onlookers.

"How are we going to do this?" the beithir asked.

"Ehm..." Macey didn't actually know. This was all one big fumble in the dark.

Amber smiled grimly. "Let's try this. I'll charge the air around us with electricity, that will make it easier for you. All you'll have to do is gather that power and discharge it into lightning."

That didn't sound too hard. Still, it took Macey at least ten tries until she managed to create a small, pitiful lightning bolt which barely reached the ground before disintegrating.

Amber laughed. "I don't think this is your strongest element."

Macey joined her laughter, glad the beithir was distracted enough not to think about her missing boyfriend. "No, I doubt that. I just don't feel the magic the same way I feel my own. It's strange, like it's a foreign object in my magic, if that makes sense."

The beithir nodded. "Maybe try combining the lightning with your water magic? That might make it stronger. Water conducts electricity."

Macey hadn't thought of that before, but it made sense.

Amber charged the air again and Macey felt the familiar tickle on her skin. She focused on her tattoos, reaching for the lightning power embedded in one of them. This probably wasn't the actual place her new elemental magic resided, but it made it easier for her to focus on it.

This time, she also pulled some of her normal water magic, and activated both of them at the same time. A lightning bolt tore through the air, strong enough to make her hair stand up.

"Yes!" Amber shouted in delight. "That's it!"

Macey grinned and created another lightning bolt. This time, the air wasn't charged as much, but it ended up being still slightly larger than the very first one she'd made.

"Now you just have to do this another hundred times or so," Amber said with an evil grin. "By then you should have a feeling for the magic."

Macey sighed. The beithir was probably right, but she didn't really like this magic. It felt wrong, especially when combined with her water magic.

"Are there any other ways I can use lightning?" she asked, hoping to distract Amber. Her eyes had begun to grow sad again.

"Well, sometimes I use thunder to scare people," Amber said with a shrug. "If you want to distract someone, create some thunder close to their head. They'll shriek and forget whatever they were about to do. I did that all the time as a child, until I almost burst someone's eardrums and my father forbid me to do it ever again." She grinned. "Not that I listened to that."

"Rebellious teenager?" Macey asked, remembering her own teenage years. She'd got up to a lot of mischief.

Amber smiled. "Something like that. That was until they sent me to Ben Veir though." She shuddered a little and Macey quickly changed the topic. She'd heard how other students had bullied Amber there and she really didn't want to open old wounds.

"Okay then, teach me how to do thunder," she said instead.

"This will sound weird, but just imagine two clouds and squeeze them together with as much force as you can."

"Seriously? Imagine clouds?"

"That's what I do," Amber said apologetically. "I don't think I can describe it any differently. It just happens. I learned it as a child so it's kind of instinctive."

Well, that didn't help.

Macey did what Amber had said, imagining clouds, but nothing happened whatsoever. Her magic wasn't based on imagining things that weren't there. Maybe thunder was a project for another day.

"Let's do some more lightning," she said with a sigh and to prove her point, created a tiny lightning bolt which singed the ground.

It took a couple more attempts for Macey to be able to conjure lightening along with her water magic. But now, she watched the two dance together, entwined as if they should have always been as one.

"Try adding another?" Amber suggested.

Macey nodded, trying to think what would work best.

"Fire," Amber whispered. "You can control it already and it is similar to lightening. You should be able to add it easily enough."

Macey's stomach cramped tightly as she considered summoning fire. When she'd been waking her markings up, she'd hastily put out her flames as she was too worried about them consuming her again. The last thing she wanted was to bring down destruction on their camp just because she'd got cocky.

Still, Amber was suggesting it and if the beithir could get past what Macey did with fire, then she could too. She closed her eyes for a brief second and pulled the fire to the surface. Holding back so it didn't all come out at once, she fed it into the lightening and water spiral, spinning it around so the three elements plaited themselves together.

"It's beautiful," Amber whispered, an ever so slight hint of envy tainting her voice.

Macey's gaze snapped to the beithir, who just shrugged.

"Wouldn't you be envious if I was the one creating this?" She waved her hand towards the beautiful tunnel of elements.

"I'm sorry, I don't know why..."

"It's fine. I'm not jealous, just having a little bit of envy. You make a lot of sense. You have Air, three of the other Wardens are your mates. It makes perfect sense for it to be you. Plus, being the hero sounds kind of exhausting."

"Isn't being the best friend exhausting too?" she teased.

Amber laughed, sounding a lot lighter than she had before. "I think it's safe to say we're all exhausted. But we're also all determined. We can take the worst the Mahoun throws at us and still be stood up fighting. But you know that, or we wouldn't still be stood by your side."

"Mmhmm." Macey nodded quickly, trying to ignore the guilt over Izban. He'd agreed to do his part after all, she really had nothing to feel bad about. If she kept telling herself that, then maybe she'd start believing it.

"I know you know where he is, Macey."

"What?" she snapped, the elemental plait dropping into nothingness along with her shock.

"Get the magic going again," Amber instructed. "But also, I wasn't sure until you just confirmed it. But you need to be able to keep control of your magic no matter what is thrown at you. If one statement from me can do it, then you're not good enough."

Macey focused for a moment, pulling out her water magic first before adding the lightning and finally the fire. "How did you work it out?" she asked once she was sure the magic was stable again.

"You didn't say anything this morning. And you're not that good of a liar either. I could see it in the way you were sitting."

"You're observant."

"And I know you well enough."

"I don't understand. If you know, then why are you still here?"

Amber sighed and sat down, indicating that Macey should too. "Keep the magic going though. And maybe add a fourth one."

"Got you," Macey muttered, conjuring up Air to

do her worst. The threads switched places, separating and turning into two threads entwined around one another.

"I know you and I know Izban. For the two of you to have agreed to something, I know it had to have been necessary for all of us."

"It is," Macey confirmed.

"It doesn't mean I'm happy about it though. Or that I'll ever forgive you if something happens to him," she warned.

"I wouldn't expect you to," Macey replied.

"And I'm sure it would be the same if the positions were reversed. Add another."

Macey nodded, calling on earth and adding it into the mix. Controlling the magic was harder now. She could feel it draining her far quicker than she wanted it to. Regardless, she kept it going. She didn't want to disappoint Amber more than she already had today.

"You're doing well," the beithir noted.

"I'm not sure I can do anything with the magic though." Her words came out through gritted teeth as she tried to keep her concentration. This was a lot harder than she wanted it to be.

"Of course you can." Amber looked around, probably searching for some kind of target. "What about that tree over there?"

"What do you want me to do with it?" Macey asked, eyeing it up from where she was sitting.

"Chop it down? Though really anything will do right now." Amber shrugged.

"Why aren't you asking me where he is?" Macey blurted.

"Two reasons," Amber answered, holding up two fingers so she could tick them off. "Firstly, if I needed to know, you'd have told me. I trust you. I trust him. Which means I don't *need* to know yet. And secondly, given where we are, there's only one place for him to be. And don't think the others won't have worked it out too by now."

"I'm sure they have," Macey replied, thinking back to Luc's knowing look. None of the men were stupid, they'd have figured it out.

"Stop stalling. Chop down the tree."

"I don't think this combination of magic is going to be good at chopping," Macey countered.

"You can't say that until you've tried. Tree." She pointed at the thing and gave Macey a stern look.

With a sigh, Macey diverted her attention, thinking on how she might achieve the impossible. The magic swayed as she tried to direct it and failed miserably. That wouldn't do. She needed to control it better but didn't know where to start.

Water. The answer was always going to be the water. She kept her mind focused on all the elements, trying to keep them together, but sent most of her focus into the strand of water magic.

Coiling it around, she directed that towards the trunk.

It almost worked. The moment the water hit the bark, she let go of some of her concentration and the elements all crashed into force. Before she could stop it, the tree burst into flames and burned to a crisp before their eyes.

"Oops."

TWELVE

After their training, Macey lay down for a nap. She was exhausted, her magic drained more than she'd anticipated. If she was to be ready to fight soon, she needed to recuperate a little.

Rónàn joined her in bed, but all he did was wrap an arm around her shoulders, providing a hard but warm pillow. She snuggled against him and fell asleep almost immediately.

MACEYYYYYYYY!

The Voice was gentle, coaxing, alluring. She wanted to follow it, do whatever it wanted her to do. Please it in any way she could.

COME TO ME, LITTLE KELPIE.

She moved towards him, becoming faster the closer she got.

THAT'S RIGHT, COME TO ME.

The Voice chuckled sweetly and Macey found it to be one of the prettiest sounds she'd ever heard. She needed to be close to it, bathe in its warmth.

She ran, following the pull she felt in her heart, racing towards the beautiful Voice. She didn't know what would happen once she got there, but she knew it was all she'd ever wanted.

GIVE YOURSELF TO ME.

Yes, that's what she wanted. He was the only one she wanted. Right?

Suddenly, she stumbled and fell, images flashing through her mind. Men, four of them. It took her a moment to identify them - but then, memories rushed over her like a bucket of cold water, waking her from her trance. Her men. Cam, Jared, Flint and Rónàn. What the waves was she doing? Why was she running towards a Voice she didn't know? Was she going mad?

DON'T THINK OF THEM. COME TO ME.

Somehow, he didn't seem as alluring anymore. She wasn't sure if she really wanted to go to him. Why was she doing it, anyway? What was awaiting her? He'd never told her why he wanted her to come.

"What do you want from me?" she called, her voice shaking a little. The warm feeling her belly had dissipated.

I WILL TELL YOU WHEN YOU'RE HERE.

She had to fight to not be convinced by his beautiful Voice. It was so tempting to just give in and do what he wanted.

"No, tell me now!"

INSOLENT CHILD!

Suddenly, he sounded a lot less enticing. He was not a nice person, was he? She turned and walked back to where she'd come from, wherever that was. Everything was a little fuzzy in her mind; she was having trouble concentrating.

DON'T! COME BACK!

She didn't turn and walked away, somehow proud of herself for whatever reason.

MACEY WOKE with a squeak that made her embarrassed as soon as her brain switched on and registered the sound she'd made.

"Everything okay?" Rónàn asked, looking at her with a trace of concern.

"Just a bad dream," she muttered, wrapping herself around him. She needed to feel him close. The last remaining tendrils of her dream were still swirling around her mind. An ominous feeling settled within her, like something bad was about to happen.

"Want me to kiss it better?" He grinned and placed a tiny kiss on her forehead.

"I wish we had the time," she whispered, kissing him on the cheek in return. "But I don't think we can do this now. Later, once we're done with kicking the Mahoun's slimy arse."

"Slimy arse?" Rónàn laughed. "I like that. I'm going to use that expression from now on."

Macey smiled. "Go ahead, it's yours."

"The devil's slimy arse is mine? Well, thank you, I guess. Nobody has ever given me someone's behind before."

A giggle broke from her throat, dispelling the last remnants of the dream.

She ran her hands over his back, admiring the hard muscle hiding beneath his soft skin.

"I'm glad you're here," she muttered, kissing him again, this time on the lips. "I couldn't do this without you. Without any of you guys."

"I'm kind of honoured to be here," he admitted. "I'm not one of the Wardens, yet you treat me like one of you."

She laughed. "You're an honorary Warden. Maybe we should change it from seven to eight. We're the last generation of Wardens anyway, nobody will mind."

"Does that mean there will be no more trouble in the world after we're gone?" he asked. "Or will the world be defenceless from new evil?"

Macey was spared from answering by shouts coming from the tent.

"Get up! Someone's approaching the camp!" Cam shouted from outside, moments before the tent flap burst open and all three of Macey's men came inside.

"Is it Izban?" Macey asked, sitting up, not caring that her boobs were on display.

Jared licked his lips at the sight, but didn't comment.

"We don't think so," Cam explained. "But whoever it is, we need you out there."

She nodded and jumped out of bed, putting on her clothes as fast as she could. Rónàn was doing the same, and she couldn't help but shoot an admiring glance at his naked body. If only they had time. They never did.

They hurried outside where the rest of their army was waiting for them.

Amber was standing a little bit removed from them, watching the horizon, where a lone figure was slowly approaching. They were walking and had reached the point about halfway between the Mahoun's castle and their camp.

"Did he come from the castle?" Macey asked.

One of the kelpies nodded. "He didn't come from the main gate though, but from a smaller door in the wall that we hadn't noticed before. He's very slow, maybe he's injured."

"Why do you say he? Couldn't it be a woman?"

The kelpie shrugged. "Yes, perhaps. I can't see them well enough from here."

Macey couldn't, either. The person was humanoid and wrapped in black clothes, but that was all she could make out. Somehow, she didn't think it was Izban though. The mage always walked with a certain swagger, and unless he was injured and couldn't walk like he normally did, it had to be someone else.

"Where's Luc?" Macey asked, noticing the daimon wasn't there with them.

"Flew off, said it was important," Flint said. "He was doing his mysterious thing again."

"Does he ever do anything else?" Macey muttered, frustration building in her. It would have been great to have Luc here just now. He could have flown towards the mysterious figure and check them out. Now, the only person with wings was Amber, and she hated putting her friend in danger. Putting the daimon in danger, not so much.

"Amber?" Macey called and the beithir turned. "Do you think it's Izban?"

"No, I'm pretty sure it isn't," Amber replied, confirming Macey's thoughts. "Want me to check it out?"

"Yes. Shall I come with you?"

Amber grimaced. She didn't like having people fly on her back.

"No, it's alright, I'll manage. If I need help, I'll create some lightning above me."

Macey nodded, smiling at her friend. "Good. We'll stand ready to assist."

Amber took off her clothes, not caring that she was naked in front of a lot of strangers, and shifted in one fluid motion. Macey always admired the ease with which the beithir could shift. For her, it was a struggle, something painful, that had to be executed perfectly in order to keep the pain to a minimum. For Amber, it seemed like an intuitive, easy thing.

The beithir leapt into the air and flew towards the castle, quickly leaving the camp behind. Macey shielded her eyes with one hand, making sure not to look away from Amber for even a second. She didn't want anything to happen to her.

"She'll be fine," Rónàn said from behind her, putting his hands on her shoulders and beginning to massage them gently. Immediately, some of her tension waned.

"What if it's a trick?" Macey asked. "It could be the Mahoun."

"Or it could be someone who wants to help," Flint said, joining Macey's side. "We'll find out in a moment. Look, Amber's almost there."

He was right. The beithir was slowly descending, drawing circles over the lone figure. If they were talking, then Macey couldn't hear it. Amber seemed relaxed, her body not curled up in a defensive position.

Suddenly, the beithir dived and wrapped her long body around the person, helping them climb onto her back. This had to be someone friendly, otherwise she'd never do that. Amber turned and flew back towards the camp, even quicker now than she'd flown before.

A minute later, she landed and a man slid from her back, wavering, then crumpling to the ground. Amber shifted faster than the eye could see.

"He needs help!" she shouted. "He's injured."

One of the kelpie healers ran forward and dropped onto his knees by the man's side, turning him onto his back. This was the first time Macey got a look at his face.

"What the..."

"Yes," Amber said, smiling grimly. "That's what I thought too. But it's not him. It's his brother."

"Malan's got a brother?" Macey exclaimed, staring at the familiar face. He looked exactly like the prophet, except that he had a body and well, he wasn't a ghost.

"Did he say anything?" she asked Amber.

"Just his name. Talon. He was about to pass out, so I thought I'd better bring him here before he died on me."

The kelpie healer was running his hands over the man's prone form.

"What's wrong with him?" Macey asked him, kneeling on Talon's other side. The man really looked like Malan. They had to be twins.

"Exhaustion, dehydration, some wounds that have festered," the healer reported, not stopping his work. "He's been tortured."

"How do you know?" Talon was wearing thick black clothes that didn't show any skin besides his face and hands.

The healer didn't even turn to look at her. "I can feel his injuries. There are a lot of old scars and wounds that never properly healed. There are broken bones, too. He must have been in incredible pain."

"When will he wake up?"

The healer frowned. "I can probably wake him now, but he will be in pain. You'll only have a few minutes, then I'll let him sleep again.

She nodded. They had to talk to him, it was imperative that they found out where Talon came from and why he was here. How he could help, preferably.

"Stand back, please," the healer commanded and Macey got back on her feet, looking down at them curiously. Of course she'd seen kelpie healers in action, many times, but she was still fascinated by their magic.

Being able to heal was something she would have loved to be able to do, but it was a magic that was very different from her own and not linked to any elements.

With a gasp, Talon suddenly woke, his eyes wide open.

His whole body twitched and shook. The healer hurriedly murmured words and Macey could almost feel the magic flowing from him into Talon. Slowly, the injured man stilled and his breathing slowed. He looked around, shock and fear evident in his expression.

"Who's in charge?" he asked with a raspy voice that clearly hadn't been used in a long time.

"I am," Macey said confidently and kneeled in front of him so that he didn't have to look up at her. "I'm Macey, one of the Seven Wardens."

"Kelpie?"

Macey nodded.

"He wants you," Talon muttered. "He's been talking about you."

"Who has?"

"The devil. He's fixated on you. On the others, too, but mostly on you."

"The devil?" Macey asked. "The Mahoun?"

Talon nodded weakly. "I've been his prisoner for years. He made me his confidant, the person he talks to when he gets bored. He gets bored a lot."

"How did you get away?"

The man sighed. "I don't know who he was. A man with blue hair. Young. Didn't say anything, just unlocked my cell door. He said the guards were dead, so I decided to try my luck at escaping. Most of the other prisoners were too weak or scared to even try."

He coughed and the healer handed him a glass of water, which he downed in one large gulp.

"How long were you there?" Macey asked, wondering whether Malan knew that his brother had been in the Mahoun's dungeons. Why hadn't the prophet done anything about it?

"I don't know, time flows differently there. It's been hard to keep track. There was war on Earth when I was captured. People wore different clothes from the ones you're wearing. Women wore dresses, not trousers like you."

"In that war, how did people fight?" Cam asked before Macey could. "What kind of weapons did they use?"

Talon looked confused. "Swords, bows, lances. Trebuchets, sometimes. Lots of metal armour."

Macey turned and exchanged looks with her men. That sounded a lot like the middle ages. Talon hadn't been a prisoner for years, he'd been captive for centuries. Maybe they shouldn't tell him that just yet.

"If you got out, does that mean we might be able to get in?" She tried not to put too much hope into her words. This might be the moment they'd waited for. Once this was over, she was going to hug Izban and forgive him all his snide words.

"I think so," Talon muttered, his voice growing weaker. "I'm sorry, I..."

His eyes closed and he stilled.

"That's enough," the healer said, looking exhausted. "I need him unconscious for the next bit, it would hurt him too much. Setting bones is not a nice affair."

Macey nodded and got up, turning to the other Wardens. Amber had dressed again, looking both excited and proud of her boyfriend.

"It seems this may be our chance," Macey said. "Are we ready?"

Cam nodded. "As ready as we can be. Everyone is rested and has been fed. All we need are orders of what to do."

Easier said than done. Everyone was looking at Macey again, waiting for her to tell them what to do. When did she become the chief strategist? She didn't know anything about war and battles. Kelpies were a peaceful species, despite the legends.

"Cam, you will lead the kelpies through that hidden door, if it's still open. One of the kabouters will come with you and assess whether the wards inside the earth have been lifted. If they have, you can mentally tell Flint, who will be waiting here with the other kabouters, ready to attack from below. Amber, you're our eyes in the sky."

"What about me?" Jared and Rónàn asked at the same time.

Macey smiled at them. "You're with me."

Illustration: The Mahoun

She shook the whole way up to the castle walls despite knowing this was what she had to do. Rónàn and Jared behind her gave her slight reassurance but not much. She loved them unconditionally but they had no idea what the Mahoun was truly capable of. Monster didn't cut it.

"MAHOUN!" she shouted before she lost her nerves and gave in to the desire to run back to the tents and disappear into her men's arms. The temptation was immense but she knew that wasn't the stuff heroes were made of. Like it or not, Luc's words had stuck and she found herself wanting to impress him. Even if he did seem to disappear at pivotal moments.

There was no answer, which didn't surprise her. She hadn't expected one quite so soon. Instead, she waited in silence, hoping her presence would be enough. He'd come to her in the dream after all. It wasn't like he didn't know she was outside the gates.

"Do you need to call again?" Rónàn asked.

Macey shook her head. "I doubt it. He's not the kind to need telling twice."

"Is this really where he kept you?" There was a hint of something unknown in Jared's voice but Macey didn't study it too hard. She didn't want to accept it could be pity.

"Yes."

"I'm sorry."

"Not your fault."

"We should have protected you better..."

"Jared," she snapped. "Me being caught had nothing to do with anything the three of you did, and you know it. Don't make this more difficult than it is. Please?" The last word came out more like a plea than the rest of it. She didn't want to beg but she couldn't have his doubt and guilt creeping in to this. For all she knew, that could be what created the Mahoun and his like in the first place.

She averted her attention back to the grand gates on the castle walls, urging the Mahoun to appear in some way, even if it was just as the Voice. She wouldn't admit it to anyone, but there was a part of her that didn't think they could defeat something that didn't even inhabit a body.

"Can I ask a question?"

"Yes?" She turned her head slightly in Rónàn's direction but didn't take her eyes off the gates. She didn't trust the Mahoun and he'd no doubt appear the moment she wasn't paying any attention.

"You sent Izban in there, didn't you?"

"No," she replied truthfully. "Izban is there of his own free will." A statement which could be construed in a few different ways. She didn't want to openly admit anything in case unfriendly ears were listening.

Both men stayed silent, no doubt each processing their own interpretation of her words. She knew they trusted her, so it didn't even matter what conclusion they came to. She just hoped it wouldn't backfire on them all. If Izban died, it would change everything. And not in a good way.

The door still stayed resolutely shut. She turned over ideas of what to do in her head but came up with nothing. Hopefully the silence on the Mahoun's part didn't mean he'd discovered the others.

"Any clues on what we need to do?" Jared asked.

"A blood sacrifice?" The suggestion was only half a joke but she didn't say that. It likely wasn't appropriate.

"Probably best not, for all we know he has a dearg-due in his employ."

Macey snorted. "I don't think he has any one in his employ, never mind an Irish woman."

"Not a woman, a dearg-due, they..."

She held up her hand, stopping him from continuing with what he was saying. "And if we believed everything from folklore, you wouldn't be with us. Give the dearg-due the same respect." She wasn't quite sure she believed that, but never having met one of the cursed blood drinkers, she didn't want to jump to any conclusions.

And she was right about Jared's kind. They weren't well received. Particularly the women.

"MAHOUN!" she shouted again, echoing the call in her mind. Hopefully that would work though she was prepared to have to do something more drastic if needed. So long as it didn't involve spilling her blood. While she stood by what she'd said about the dearg-due, she didn't want to take the chance of blood magic being used against them.

YOU CALLED, LITTLE KELPIE?

The Voice reverberated around her mind and she shuddered. She might have wanted him to appear, but now he had, she wasn't completely sure about that.

"You wanted me to come to you, well here I am." She held out her arms, not caring how dramatic it made her look.

Or how crazy. She had no idea if Jared and Rónàn could hear the Voice too.

BUT NOT ALONE.

"Even if I was, I wouldn't be alone."

THAT'S WHAT YOU THINK.

Macey didn't answer. She knew she'd never convince him. Just like she knew she was right. Her heart would never be alone, no matter what he said.

"What do you want from me?" Her voice shook despite her attempts not to let it.

TOTAL SUBMISSION.

"That's not an option."

THEN MAKE IT ONE.

A sensation like she'd never experienced before flooded through her body and she tried to push it away. She wouldn't let him have the upper hand. She couldn't let him. He was the Mahoun, the person they were trying to destroy. He couldn't be allowed to gain the upper hand. She would resist him if it was the last thing she did, while hoping it wasn't.

"Why won't you come out and face us?" she demanded.

Jared reached out and placed a comforting hand on her back. Rónàn did the same on the other side. She leaned back into their touches, their support filling her with strength she'd been missing before.

YOU AND YOUR ARMY?

His laughter reverberated throughout her. He really didn't believe they were any kind of threat. That would be his undoing if he wasn't careful. If there was one thing she'd learned, it was that underestimating anyone was a bad move. But then, wasn't she doing the same by not believing his threats?

She frowned but said nothing. Her head was in knots as it was. She didn't want to make it worse.

WHAT HAS YOUR ARMY GOT THAT I HAVEN'T, LITTLE KELPIE?

She thought through the people assembled around the foot of the castle and came back with nothing. They were just a gaggle of people brought together for a common cause and nothing more. She didn't even know how some of them would fare in a battle situation. She hoped well, but there was no way of truly knowing. And if she was honest, she was in no rush to find out. Battle meant death. Having anyone's on her conscious wasn't what she wanted in life.

Thoughts of Izban flitted through her mind but she squashed them down again. The last thing she wanted was the Voice to work out what she was up to.

The booming laugh returned, making her jump as the shock overtook her. She really didn't like it when he did that.

THE ICE WARDEN? YOU STILL HOPE HE'S ON YOUR SIDE, DON'T YOU?

She didn't answer, but doubts started to creep in as he spoke. She was still hoping Izban was on their side and that she hadn't just handed him the tools to betray them all. She couldn't think about it now, there was still time before she'd know which side he was on for sure.

"We can take you with or without Izban." She wasn't completely sure she was telling the truth, but she had to believe it or else he'd sense her indecision.

She could feel the Voice's disbelief but ignored it. There was nothing else she could do about it other than stand her ground. There was a great deal of confusion about the situation though. Why was the Voice being so passive? He'd wanted Macey to come to him but now she had, he was doing nothing with her.

YOU WILL COME WITH ME.

"Why should I?"

The Voice laughed again. What was it about this time? He wasn't doing anything she'd consider to be laugh worthy.

Choking sounds sounded from behind her and the two men's hands fell away from Macey's back. Panicked, she spun around and took in the sight of the two of them clutching their throats and desperate for breath.

"STOP!" she screamed. "I'll come with you."

ALONE?

"I don't see that you've left me with much choice," she replied begrudgingly.

GOOD.

The choking stopped and Macey sighed in relief.

She reached out to Rónàn but the Mahoun's presence in her mind stopped her. She shivered. He hadn't been able to reach out like that in a while.

COME.

The doors to the Keep creaked open, leading into the darkness beyond.

Without saying a word, she turned away from her men and stepped towards certain danger. She couldn't bring herself to care though. As if the Voice hadn't done enough already, he was now actively threatening her men's lives. Not that he hadn't been before, but it felt more personal now and she wasn't about to have that.

The walk between their spot and the doors was surprisingly lengthy, and yet it took no time at all. She didn't look back. If she did, she'd lose her conviction and run back to safety. Or perceived safety at any rate. In reality, there was no real safe haven while the Mahoun lived on.

The doors slammed shut behind her, leaving her completely blind. Still, she walked on, eager to get to where she needed to be and face what she had to. The sooner this was over, the better as far as Macey was concerned.

Turning a corner, she stepped into a pool of light and had to shield her eyes, a slight cry of alarm leaking from her. The very tips of her fingers tingled as the magic inside urged to be released. It could sense the danger around them no doubt, but she wasn't ready to unleash it and let it play. She was still hoping that the Mahoun hadn't realised she held the powers of all seven elements yet. Even if he only suspected, she wanted to keep him in the dark for as long as possible.

She stepped out of the light and back into the thick black darkness around them. There was a part of her which was convinced this was nothing more than an illusion.

I'VE BEEN WONDERING, MACEY...

The Voice was almost pleasant again, seductive even. She said nothing. She wouldn't give in to his call even if she wanted to.

CAN YOU FIND ME THROUGH THE MEMORIES?

She braced herself, unsure about what she would be faced with. Would he throw memories of her childhood at her or something more sinister? Her time here even?

Cries started up as soon as she had that thought but the sounds weren't ones she recognised. These were the screams of innocents. Fellow victims of the Voice who hadn't managed to escape like she had. Her heart sank. Could she cope with the torture reaching her ears? She could swear there were even the cries of children hidden among the pain.

She soldiered on, trying to ignore the distractions. There was no time to dwell on this. People still living needed her more than the dead did at this point.

"I'm sorry," she whispered, only then realising that tears were falling quickly down her cheeks. If she could have seen properly, she was sure they'd have splashed against the floor too.

She turned another corner, the darkness still thick around her. This time, there was light at the end though, and not the blinding light of earlier either. It was softer, more like firelight.

If only that was reassuring. After her time with the lampads, she doubted she'd ever find fire comforting again. Unless it was coming from Flint that was.

Stepping into the light, her vision returned slowly and she noticed a single black clad figure in the middle of the room, a hood covering his head and features.

She wasn't sure how she knew, but this was definitely the Mahoun. Or as human as the Mahoun got.

I'M IMPRESSED.

"You should be," she responded, not having any more time for his games. She could still hear the faint cries of the people he'd tortured but was just about managing to block them out. A small kernel of guilt grew in her stomach over that. She shouldn't be ignoring those in pain. She was a Warden. It was her job to protect the world and all that lived in it, no matter the cost to herself.

Holding on to that thought as tightly as she could, she straightened her spine and met the Mahoun's invisible gaze.

"What do you want from me?" she demanded.

EVERYTHING.

"How specific," she muttered, unimpressed by his evil speech giving skills. Wasn't this where he was supposed to monologue his entire plot to her while she created a mad plan of her own that somehow worked despite all the odds?

She'd been reading too many books.

YOU WILL SURRENDER THE WARDENS TO ME.

"I'm sorry, I can't do that. I'm only one of them," she pointed out.

LIES.

"Fine. Two."

LIES.

"Truth," she countered, putting as much conviction in her voice as she possibly could. He wasn't beating her this way.

THAT'S NOT HOW THE WARDENS WORK.

"It is as far as I'm aware." She stepped further forward, almost gasping in shock when a face behind the Mahoun was revealed to her.

Luc held a finger to his lips. She didn't know why he was here, or even if he was a friend in this situation, but she obeyed. If he really was here to help her, then she'd take it. She'd need every little bit of help she could possibly get.

The Mahoun laughed in her head. It was disconcerting being able to see him but the hooded figure wasn't moving when he spoke or cackled. She had to wonder if this was really him or if it was just another ruse.

Something deep within her was convinced that wasn't the case though. She was in the presence of pure evil and her body and soul knew it.

HOW ARE YOUR FIGHTING SKILLS?

"What?" she blurted before she had time to think.

The Mahoun moved sharply, a duelling cane leaping into his hands. He twirled it around, looking every inch the deadly foe he was.

Macey gulped loudly, she didn't have anything she could use to combat that.

Luc caught her eye and threw her a cane of her own. Trusting in her reflexes and her magic, she opened up her hand and caught the staff. It was perfectly weighted, as if it had been made for her.

DAIMON!

The Voice sounded enraged, but the Mahoun still moved towards Macey, evil intent in every movement.

Luc moved into the light so he was standing next

to Macey, a staff of his own in his hands. Confidence flooded through her. With both of them there, maybe they stood a chance. Though with their opponent being an evil being of immense power, that might have been a stretch still.

"Do you know what you're doing with that?" Luc whispered to her.

Macey shook her head. "My plan was to trust in my magic."

"Good. You're learning then."

"Do you?" She nodded towards his cane.

He didn't answer out loud, instead he spun it around in much the same way the Mahoun had. Good. That meant they really might stand a chance.

The Voice cackled more in her head, probably already confident of victory. No matter what she did or how hard he fought, Macey was determined not to let him have that.

She steeled her heart, pulling on the strength of her bonds with the other Wardens. They wouldn't feel anything on their end but it gave her the extra protection and skills she would need.

It was time to see if they were Wardens in more than just name. In a way that had nothing at all to do with magic.

FOURTEEN

The fight had become an intricate dance of wooden staffs meeting with a clunk, then returning to their masters again, then meeting once more in a cacophony of sound. This wasn't a fight as much as a show of strength and confidence.

Luc was in his element, easily blocking the Mahoun's attacks, but Macey was beginning to think that the devil was just toying with them. Maybe he was even trying to distract them while he had a much worse plan put into action by his lackeys.

Hopefully, the others had entered the castle and were following the plan.

Slightly distracted, Macey lost her grip on her magic and the Mahoun's staff got through her defences, knocking hard against her shoulder. She stumbled back, cursing herself for her carelessness. She didn't know how to fight, but somehow, her magic did. She just had to keep connected to it. She ignored the aching pain flaring down her arm and filled herself with magic once more, letting herself be led by it. She stepped forward and attacked the Mahoun in new fervour, joining Luc's ever faster strokes. Together, they matched the Mahoun, but neither he nor they were getting the upper hand.

She still didn't know why he'd chosen to do this little staff fight. He could have just slipped into her mind again and fought her there. No, instead he was fighting her physically. There had to be a reason for it, but she couldn't stop to think.

She blocked his next attack, then swooped low and aimed for his feet, but he twisted his staff faster than she could see and prevented her from succeeding. Something needed to change; this was a waste of time.

From the corners of her eyes, she glanced at Luc. The daimon was fighting hard, his wings steadying him, half unfolded. She was surprised his long black cloak didn't get in the way.

THIS IS FUN, the Mahoun shouted in Macey's mind.

"No, it isn't!" she called back in between blocking yet another vicious attack. "What do you want?"

YOU.

"Could you be more specific?"

I TOLD YOU. I WANT YOU TO SUBMIT TO ME. I WANT YOU TO BE MINE.

Macey decided she was done with the staff and let it drop to the floor, creating a coil of magic instead.

"Dream on," she hissed while weaving together lightning, water and fire magic, keeping it invisible so the Mahoun wouldn't see what she was doing. Luc was continuing to block the man's attacks, now having to protect both himself and Macey.

BY THE END OF TODAY, YOU'LL WISH YOU'D GIVEN IN EARLIER.

A shiver ran over her back. No, that wasn't going to happen. She wasn't going to let him scare her. Not that she wasn't scared shitless already, but she wasn't going to let him make it worse. Right now, he looked like a man and a man could be killed. He was no longer the disembodied Voice, but flesh and blood.

Suddenly, the Mahoun broke through Luc's defences and hit the daimon hard on the knee. Luc screamed and fell to the ground, his staff slipping from his hand.

Macey had to act, now, before the Mahoun hurt Luc. She took the magic coil and flung it at the Mahoun like she had at the tree when they were practicing earlier that day. The tree had burst into flame. The Mahoun... he laughed.

NICE TRICK, BUT ABSOLUTELY USELESS ON ME.

She stared at where her magic used to be. Sparks were falling down, her magic, disintegrated. She'd thought she was strong, but he had defended himself against her attack without even moving. How the fucking waves did he do that?

Ignoring her, he lifted his staff, ready to let it pummel down on Luc. No, she couldn't let that happen.

Instead of carefully planning her next attack, she simply threw random magic at the Mahoun, whatever she could find within herself. A lance of water hit him in the stomach, or at least it would have, had he not had some kind of invisible shield surrounding him. The water she'd thrown at him was now a useless puddle on the ground, soaking his black boots.

That gave her an idea. She formed a very big, very obvious flame and then pushed it towards him, giving him time to completely focus on it, while at the same time, she created some lightning and made it hit the wet ground beneath his feet.

He screamed as lightning raced through his body, making his limbs twitch.

Macey poured more energy into the lightning, creating more and more bolts that she fired at the Mahoun. His guards were down while he tried to deal with the pain she was causing him.

Luc groaned and she turned to him, her eyes widening when she saw how his leg was bent in an unnatural angle. That hit had to have been a lot more violent than it had looked. He grabbed his staff and threw it at Macey, who just about managed to catch it.

"Blow to the head," Luc shouted over the Mahoun's screams. "Get him unconscious."

Macey took two steps towards the cloaked man and lifted the staff, bringing it down on the back of his head with as much force as she could muster. The screaming stopped and he collapsed into a heap.

As soon as he was on the ground, Macey ripped the hood off his head - and screamed. There was no face. Pale white skin was drawn over where the face was supposed to be, but it was smooth like that of a shop window mannequin. This wasn't a human being, or even a humanoid person. No, this was some kind of weird creation of the Mahoun, not the devil himself.

FIGURED IT OUT YET?

She swirled around, but there was nobody in the room besides Luc and herself.

"It was too easy," she whispered and the cackle of the Voice confirmed her suspicions.

IT'S TIME FOR A NEW GAME.

Suddenly, the room around her disappeared and she was thrown into darkness.

"HELLO?" she called out, getting to her feet. Everything was dark; no, not just normal darkness, but a thick, foggy blackness that felt both threatening and ominous. "Anyone here?"

Silence.

She conjured a flame, but before it could even illuminate the room, it flickered out. She tried again, and again, but something snuffed out her magic as soon as she created it. It reminded her of the Mahoun's dungeons, where she'd been imprisoned. It had been impossible to do magic there as well, but it felt a little different here. The magic inside her was still there, it just didn't exist anymore as soon as it left her body.

"I tried that, it doesn't work. Save your energy."

She recognised that voice, even though he hadn't sounded as exhausted the last time she'd spoken to him.

"Izban?"

"Yes, over here."

She followed the direction of his voice until she stumbled over something soft.

"Ouch," the mage complained.

"Sorry," Macey muttered, making sure not to step on him. "What happened? Are you injured?"

"Just my pride. What happened? Is Amber alright?"

Macey nodded before she realised he couldn't see her.

"Yes, at least she was last time I saw her. They're attacking the castle as we speak. I was fighting the Mahoun but, well, he turned out to be not himself."

"That doesn't make any sense," Izban said with a sigh. "But I think I know what you mean. Hooded man, no face?"

"You've seen him?" Macey asked, surprised.

"He welcomed me in, let me tell him my story, then attacked without warning. I defeated him, saw his face, heard the Voice and ended up here."

Macey sat down by his side, noticing there was a wall just behind him that he was leaning against. "Pretty much the same thing happened to me," she said. "I wonder what Luc is doing now. He was suddenly there, in the castle, and helped me fight."

"The daimon? He's a strange one."

Macey was tempted to say that Izban was even stranger, but she swallowed that reply. The two of them were in this together now, and who knew when they'd see the others again.

"Talon came to the camp," she said instead. "He said you let him out of his cell."

"The old man?" Izban asked. "Was it just me or does he look like Malan."

Macey chuckled. "He said he's his brother. And yes, I find that just as weird as you do."

"Weird doesn't even cover it," Izban muttered, then fell quiet.

Macey kicked at the wall, frustrated that they couldn't seem to get out.

"I tried that."

"Yes, I imagined you would have," she snapped.

"How did you escape last time?" he asked.

"Didn't Amber tell you?"

"No. She doesn't talk about her time here."

"Not surprising," Macey muttered under her breath. It wasn't like she'd been particularly forthcoming about her time in the Voice's Keep either. Far from it. "We won't be getting out the same way," she added.

"Why not?"

"Because the Mahoun doesn't make mistakes like that twice." Her patience with the man was already running thin. Though that was true of her patience with him all the time. She wasn't too sure what it was about him but Izban really rubbed her up the wrong way. She was just glad fate hadn't decided he was to be one of her men too. That would have been too much.

"So what do you suppose we do?"

"I don't know." She grunted in frustration. How had she managed to get herself here again? Once wasn't enough for her, she just came running back to the Mahoun's grasp. Stupid. Stupid. Stupid.

"Will the others help?"

"I don't know if they can." She bit her words out through gritted teeth as she tried to think. There must be some way of getting out of here. She couldn't let herself be beaten by the Voice. Not at this stage in the game. She had a godsforsaken army outside.

And where was Luc? He'd been with her fighting the Mahoun, he should be here too. Except his absence must have meant something else. She wasn't naive enough to think it meant he'd gotten away. That wasn't how the Voice worked.

Unless...

He'd managed to get into the castle undetected. Maybe the Mahoun wasn't actually able to sense the daimon. Not unless someone talked to him. The fight was different, he'd physically been attacking. Maybe the Mahoun had just thought she was using her magic to fight like that...

She shook her head. Idle thoughts like that weren't going to get her anywhere. Not when the whole reason she was having them was because she didn't want to accept the truth. The Mahoun had them. If she didn't do something about it soon, then they were all going to die. Not just her and Izban, but everyone in her army too.

Everyone she'd brought here to end up slaughtered.

Frustrated tears began to fall from her eyes. How could she have done this? Everyone she thought of as a friend and an ally would only suffer betrayal and death. She'd go down in history as the Warden who caused nothing but death and destruction.

If there was any history left at all. There was a good chance the Voice wouldn't stop at just the people outside the walls. He wanted everyone. The whole world under his control or burning.

Flames leaped up around them and Macey jumped back.

Not Izban though. He just stood there, the flames licking at his clothing and trying to burn him whole.

"Izban?" Her voice shook as she asked.

"Had an idea?" he asked snidely.

"How are you standing in the flames?" The pieces

were already starting to slot together in Macey's mind but she wasn't entirely sure. A lot of it hinged on Izban's reply.

"Oh. I didn't realise I was." He stepped forward, leaving the fire behind him. His clothes were completely unsinged and there wasn't even a soot mark on him.

"MAHOUN!" Macey shouted at the top of her lungs. "You can let me out now."

A loud chuckle filled her head.

VERY GOOD, LITTLE KELPIE. THAT DIDN'T TAKE YOU AS LONG AS I THOUGHT.

"I'm glad I can be of amusement," she muttered, not really talking to him.

SO FIRE WON'T PHASE YOU. WHAT WILL...

The flames disappeared in an instant, collapsing in on themselves and being replaced by a white tundra. Snow flicked against Macey's skin, the hard pellets hurting with the velocity at which the wind knocked them against her.

Something clicked in her head. She was being tested by the elements. All she needed to do was break through the illusion and the Mahoun would be hers to face.

In theory.

A huddled figure caught her eye and she stumbled

towards it, knowing in her heart that it was Flint and he was in trouble. Ice and Wind couldn't be a good combination for the Fire Warden. She had to help relight his fire.

She stumbled and fell to her knees, the cold snow only increasing the sting. She needed to get to him though. Not even weather like this would stop her from helping her Warden.

Macey tried to stand but stumbled again.

No matter. She would crawl.

Forcing her hands into the cold snow, she dragged herself towards Flint, desperate to get to him and help him. If it was the last thing she did, she would manage. He was more important to her than life itself. They all were.

It took a painstakingly long time and her limbs tingled from the cold. It took everything she had to remember it was all in her head and she wasn't actually suffering from the damage she thought she was. She had to hand it to the Mahoun, this was devious. For anyone who hadn't already been victim to his mind games, it would drive them mad in a heartbeat.

"Flint?" she whispered as she reached him, her hands pressing against his rapidly cooling body. She reminded herself again that this wasn't real. That he wasn't real. But it was difficult to remember.

YOU REALLY ARE A FOOL.

She ignored the Voice, knowing what was coming next.

The snow vanished as quickly as it had arrived, taking Flint with it.

YOUR LOVE FOR THEM WILL BE YOUR UNDOING.

She didn't answer. She didn't need to. He was wrong on a lot of levels but she didn't want to tell him why. If he thought she was going to hand him the keys to destroying her, then he had another thing coming.

The space around Macey didn't change this time. It just stayed black, like she was standing in the middle of a void. With nothing around her, she didn't know which way to look.

The Voice's laugh changed, almost becoming a knowing chortle.

HAVE FUN.

She closed her eyes, but that didn't help. It was dark both inside and outside her mind.

Noises sounded around her. Noises that called long loving nights to her mind. Confused, Macey made the mistake of opening her eyes. The moment she did, she screwed them tightly shut once more, trying to block out what she'd seen.

It didn't work. Now she'd seen them, the images played behind her eyelids too. One of the disadvantages of all this happening in her head.

"Maceyyyyyyy, come and play?" Amber begged, pouting as she did.

"No thanks," she muttered, not wanting to even entertain the ideas of what she was seeing.

"But Flint's cock is lonely. Take him while I ride Jared."

"No thank you." Macey began to shake as jealousy rose within her. This was just like the lampads' test. She'd managed that, she could manage this.

She opened her eyes again, fully facing the images before her. Everyone was there. Everyone was naked and they all had eyes for Amber. Apart from Izban, who stood in the corner glaring at Macey. He would always be the one who hated her the most.

"Who should I try first, Macey? The incubus? I've heard they're better in bed when they're already sated, so maybe not."

Macey shook her head.

"No? Okay. What about the wraiths, I bet they could take me both at once. Though Camdan looks a little too sweet for that. I'm not sure he's up to the task."

She didn't reply to the apparition. This wasn't Amber, she knew that. This wasn't happening. She knew that too. It didn't stop the very real feelings inside her though.

"What about the daimon? It might be fun to have someone before you."

Macey's eyes snapped to where the apparition was circling a naked Luc. She tried not to let her gaze stray downwards but curiosity made that almost impossible. Her eyes widened. What was she even doing admiring him like that? How could she be so unfaithful to her men? The twisting in her gut wasn't easing at this suggestion from Amber though. She pushed the implications away. Now wasn't the time to deal with them and even if it was, she didn't want to. Ever.

"No? I guess that leaves the selkie first then. It's a good thing I like things wet."

Tears streaked their way down Macey's cheeks. The Voice was cruel if he wanted this to be her punishment. She knew what he wanted and it pained her to even entertain the notion.

Steeling herself, Macey met the seductive gaze of apparition Amber. It helped that she couldn't see any of her friend in that look.

She gulped loudly and begged for forgiveness for her real men.

"You can take them all, Amber. It means nothing to me."

Horror flitted across the apparition's face as the words sunk in. The darkness shrivelled and died, collapsing in on itself.

Macey was thrown to the floor once more. Her knees really were taking a pounding, but the sting and the coolness were all she needed to know this wasn't another vision. She was back in the castle properly. As if the Mahoun's receding laugh wasn't enough.

"Macey?" Luc asked softly, his hands going around her shoulders and helping her back to her feet.

She tried not to look at him, embarrassed over what the Voice had shown her.

"Are you okay?"

She nodded, not able to find any of her words.

"You're scaring me. Why are you so pale?"

"Your knee?" she croaked.

"Daimon magic. If I'm not being attacked, I can heal myself pretty quickly. It's a useful trick. But what happened?" he repeated.

"Mind games. Nothing more than mind games."

"HOW LONG WAS I OUT?" Macey asked, brushing off her clothes.

"A few minutes, long enough for me to heal myself and for the body to disintegrate. I checked on you but you looked like you were simply sleeping. Did you have fun?"

He gave her a sympathetic wink, as if he knew that humour was a good way to deal with it all.

"Oh yes, it was hilarious," she said drily, "but I met Izban. He must be somewhere around here."

"We'll find him. Let's go."

She looked at the daimon in confusion. "Aren't we locked in here?"

"What would give you that idea?" he asked while opening the door at the other end of the chamber.

"I thought we were prisoners," she muttered. "It felt that way."

He was in front of her in a flash, lifting her head with a finger on her chin until she was forced to look into his dark eyes.

"We are not prisoners. We are invaders. We are the ones attacking and we are the ones who will succeed. We are the strong people here, not the victims, understood?"

She was both confused and amazed by the passion in his voice. It really mattered to him what she thought.

After a moment, he let her go, walking back to the door.

"Come on, let's find the real Mahoun."

She followed him, leaving the strange room and entering a corridor made from a strange, smooth stone that reminded her of dark glass. There were shouts in the distance, but she wasn't able to identify any of the voices.

"They're fighting, that's a good sign," Luc said and

Macey tended to agree. Better fighting than lying dead somewhere.

They increased their pace until they were almost running through the tunnel. There were no doors that would have let them out, only an endless, straight corridor. After five minutes, Macey stopped, breathing hard.

"This tunnel can't be this long," she huffed. "The keep isn't big enough for that. We must either be underground, which also doesn't make sense because we never walked down any stairs, or this is yet another illusion."

YOU'RE TOO SLOW, the Mahoun's voice boomed in her head. YOU SHOULD HAVE NOTICED THAT AGES AGO. I'M GROWING TIRED OF PLAYING WITH YOU.

"I'm tired of you hiding from us!" Macey shouted back. "Come and show yourself! Let's fight this out face to face."

WOULDN'T YOU LIKE THAT, LITTLE KELPIE. NO, I THINK I HAVE BETTER THINGS TO DO. THERE'S AN INCUBUS TO TORTURE. HOW MUCH DO YOU THINK HE'S GOING TO MISS HIS COCK ONCE IT'S GONE? WILL HE BE ABLE TO SURVIVE?

Macey screamed in outrage and fear. This devil was not going to get his filthy fingers on her men. She was going to find him and rip out his heart.

First though, they had to get out of this tunnel. Luckily, the Voice mentioning Jared had given her an idea.

"Stand back," she warned Luc. "I've not tried this before."

She concentrated on the Earth mark on her back, hoping that would help her focus. She'd not tried to duplicate any of Jared's elemental powers before, but she didn't have time to practice. It had to work, there was no other option.

She focused on the smooth wall to her right, feeling into the stone, trying to figure out where they were and whether there was an exit somewhere. It took her a moment to make sense of the sensations her magic gave her. It all felt cold, unyielding, stoic. Like stone, basically.

Then, slowly, that feeling gave way to something else, something warmer. The Earth behind the stone. It told her stories of waiting and longing, but she didn't have time to listen. One day, she would, but not now.

Now knowing what to do, she tried what she usually did with the Staran: tell it what she needed. She focused on the image of her men, and of Amber and Izban, hoping the Earth would somehow understand. She almost chuckled at that thought. Her life really had become crazy.

To her surprise, the ground began to rumble and she was flung back, landing against something soft. Luc. As soon as the shaking stopped, she stepped away from him, a little embarrassed at the close touch. The daimon confused her immensely. She didn't know what to feel about him, around him, of him. He was a guide, she found him irritating, and yet he had a strange allure that made her want to find out more about him.

She shook her head, ridding her mind of those pesky thoughts, and turned back to the wall - which now had a giant hole in it. Finally. The magic seemed to have worked.

"Well done," Luc said, slapping her back in emphasis. "Now let's get out of here."

Without waiting, he stepped through the hole, bowing his head so he could fit through it. Macey followed, a little annoyed that he'd taken the lead even though it had been her who got them out of the never-ending corridor.

She stepped into a small cave, completely different from the clean, almost clinical tunnel they'd been in before. This looked more like a burrow, with roots clinging to the walls and an uneven ground full of what looked like mole hills.

"Who's there?" a deep voice called from the distance. She thought she recognised it, but only when the Kabouter stepped into the dim light, she realised it was one of her allies. Seppe, she thought his name was, but she wasn't quite sure.

"It's Macey!" she shouted even though he was now close enough to hear her. He was wearing leather armour like most of the Kabouters, but there was a deep gash on the front, almost ripping the leather apart. If he hadn't worn armour, his chest would have likely been cleaved in two by whatever had hit him.

"What happened?" she asked.

"Just some guards, nothing we couldn't handle," he said with pride. "But what on earth are you doing down here? Shouldn't you be up there with the others?"

"Where exactly are we?" Macey was a little embarrassed to admit that she had no idea, even though that was hardly her fault.

"About a hundred feet beneath the dungeons," Sepp explained. "I'm standing guard while the others are trying to get the prisoners out."

"Take us there," she commanded and he nodded.

"Your incubus is up there as well. He's almost as good with Earth as a Kabouter."

She grinned as she followed the gnome into yet another tunnel, this one narrow and a little smelly. It soon began to rise upwards and she had to concentrate on where she put her feet on the uneven ground. By the time they reached yet another hole that brought them out of the tunnel and into the lowest level of the castle, she was exhausted and covered in dirt.

Not ideal, should the Mahoun come to attack them again.

Sepp pointed towards the left. "Dungeons are that way. I'll go back and guard the exit."

Before she could say anything to him, he'd disappeared.

"What now?" Macey asked the daimon who'd been walking behind her. He didn't seem out of breath at all, something she was a little jealous of.

"Now we continue searching for our enemies," he said grimly. "This was a distraction aimed to buy him more time. But for what?"

It was a rhetorical question, that much was clear. Neither of them knew what the Mahoun was planning, except that it couldn't be good.

The walked silently along rows of empty cells. Either there had been no occupants, or they had been freed. There was a strange smell in the air, something sad, full of despair. Macey couldn't put her finger on what it was exactly, but she tried to breathe through her mouth to avoid it.

At the end of the large room, a door led up a narrow set of steps and into another level of the dungeon. More cells, and this time, not all of them were empty. She covered her mouth with her hands when they passed the first body, already starting to decompose.

"Don't look," Luc said softly. "There's nothing we can do."

It hurt, but she knew he was right. They were too late to help these poor buggers, but they would avenge them. Macey squared her shoulders and increased her pace. The Mahoun was going to pay, and the sooner she reached him, the better.

SIXTEEN

She could feel each of the elements bubbling up inside her, reaching to be let loose on the world and take the vengeance Macey desired for her. She held them back though, she couldn't let them go too early or else the Mahoun would know what she had in store for him far earlier than she anticipated.

"Are you okay?" Luc asked.

She glared at him out of the corner of her eye. Admittedly, it was nice not to be on her own but he was bordering on clingy with his checking in. She tried to reason with herself, pointing out that he was her guide. That gave him a right to be clingy. The success of his life's mission depended on her well being.

Her mind drifted to the vision of him with the others but she dismissed it quickly. She didn't want to think about him that way, it would only complicate matters further and blur the lines between them. She shouldn't be thinking about it at all, especially when she didn't know if her men were safe.

Stupid thought. Of course they weren't safe. All of them were in and about the Mahoun's castle. Safe wasn't something anyone was here. Danger lurked in every corner and death was an almost certainty no matter what any of them did. She was just trying to keep the death to a minimum.

"He's being quiet," Luc observed.

"It doesn't mean he's not listening," Macey returned. Chances were he was *always* listening. Privacy was a thing of the past while they were in the Mahoun's lair.

"I'm sure it doesn't."

Their footsteps echoed off the dungeon floors but otherwise, there wasn't a sound around them. The bodies surrounding them didn't stir, for which Macey wasn't sure whether to be grateful or not. They didn't seem to be anyone she knew but that hardly mattered. The Mahoun had claimed so many lives it was tragic to think of.

Shuffling started at her feet and she frowned more. "Was that you?" she demanded.

Luc shook his head. "No..."

"Then..." Her words trailed off as one of the bodies began to move. "They're alive!" Relief washed through her as she rushed to help the person to his feet.

"Macey! No!" Luc called, jumping between her and the man needing help.

"What are you..."

"Macey, look with your eyes and not your heart. I know you want them to be alive. Trust me, I want that too, but they're not."

She blinked a couple of times, trying to make sense of what he was saying and what she was seeing. It didn't make any sense.

The rest of the bodies began to shuffle about, doing weird jerking movements as they rose.

"L-luc?" Her voice shook violently as her mind tried to process what she was seeing.

"You know as much as I do." He didn't sound much steadier. "Any ideas?"

"How will they react to fire?" She shot him a glance, hoping to find some reassurance on his features.

She didn't. All she got was a hint of fear but an undercurrent of determination.

"I've no idea. But let's start with the most obvious."

As if by magic, he pulled a shimmering blade from his robes and muttered something in Greek over it. A blessing no doubt, she'd seen some of the kelpies do the same in their own language.

Luc stepped towards the figure in front of them and swung the blade around, slicing cleanly through the neck of the man limping towards them.

There was no blood. No scream. Nothing to suggest he'd been alive. Everything to terrify Macey even further. To make matters worse, his body still moved towards them, the blood and sinew of his neck a gruesome testimony to the body's previous set.

"Alright, so chopping their heads off doesn't work," she muttered, disbelief coursing through her. How had her world become like this? It was almost enough to regret every dream of adventure she'd had a small child.

"Which means that stabbing, slicing or other kinds of chopping won't work either," Luc said dryly.

"No, I don't suppose it would. What's left then?" She backed towards him as the decomposing bodies moved inwards, forming a tight circle around them. She grunted in frustration. This was like every zombie movie she'd ever seen. She made a mental note never to yell at the characters about getting into stupid situations like this again. It was only too easy to end up in one.

"Pure magic from the heavens?" Luc suggested with a shrug.

"Does that even exist?"

"How should I know? I'm a daimon, not exactly a heavenly being."

"Is heaven real?" Awe filled her at the thought.

"No. But can we do this another time? If we start chatting about the afterlife, we'll soon find out the truth for ourselves first hand."

"Can you even die?" She couldn't help the question slipping from her.

"Yes, I can die. But I don't particularly want to."

"Right. So, ideas?"

"I'm hoping we can come up with one pretty damned soon. I can fight them off but that doesn't seem to be slowing them down much."

One of the bodies stumbled towards Macey, grabbing out and trying to catch her. She threw water magic at the thing on reflex, hoping it would be enough to stop the thing in its tracks.

No such luck. She shouldn't be surprised. It wasn't like things had been going her way otherwise.

Lightening bubbled beneath her fingertips, longing to be released but she ignored it. While the magic was powerful, she could only direct it in one place at once, which was no good against the circle of dead bodies she'd found herself among.

Fire. That was the answer, even if unleashing that much power again still scared her. Knowing she had no other choice, she reached within herself and found the anger from before. She tugged it out of her heart, demanding it rise to the surface. Fiery pain lanced through her veins as the magic moved to the surface. This was it. The answer. All she needed to do was burn the bodies. A man without a head could still walk. Ash couldn't.

"Stand back!" she warned Luc and unleashed the fire. Heat streamed through her and the smell of burning flesh filled her nose. She closed her eyes, unable to keep looking at the bodies being set alight. Their skin was melting, their hair had already been burned away, yet still they advanced towards them. This magic was evil, torturing the dead even further after all they'd been through in life. In this moment, Macey really hoped there was an afterlife where these people could have a better life. Hopefully, they'd never know their bodies had been used as weapons by the Mahoun.

Luc lifted his sword, ready to defend them, but slowly, the bodies became slower as their flesh sizzled and turned into ash.

Tears were freely streaming down Macey's cheeks. In her mind, she knew she hadn't killed them, they'd already been dead, but her heart felt unbelievable loss and guilt. She was never going to be able to use this magic on living people, not after seeing and smelling what it could do. Never.

Despite the ache in her chest, she didn't stop until all of the bodies had burned into heaps of ash and bones. Bile rose up in her throat and she hunched over, retching. Luc put a hand on her lower back and a soothing tingling spread through her.

She wasn't sure if it was his magic or just his presence, but it helped get her stomach under control. She wasn't going to give up now. She couldn't be weak.

She stood and wiped her mouth.

"Let's go," she said quietly and walked away from the carnage she had caused, not looking back.

LUCKILY, the cells on the next level were empty. No more zombies for the Mahoun to resurrect. Still, they proceeded with caution, always aware that they were likely being watched. It was strange that the Mahoun hadn't tried to talk to them, or stop them. Maybe he was busy torturing Izban. Macey ground her jaw. As much as she didn't like the mage, she didn't want him to suffer either. She was one of the Wardens and as such, he was under her protection.

"I wonder how many people he's imprisoned here," Luc said after a while, staring at the endless rows of empty cells. "And why."

Macey grimaced. "Maybe not for any particular reason. He's an entity that feeds on belief, and a lot of people believe in evil, no matter the reason for it. It might be in his nature to torture and cause pain.

He doesn't need an excuse to do so. He just does it."

"I fear you may be right about that," the daimon sighed. "Let's hope the next floor is something else."

However, before they could ascend the steps at the end of the room, a noise to their right made them turn. There was someone in one of the cells.

Macey stepped forward, but then remembered the dead bodies from before and stayed where she was, ready to throw some magic at whoever this was.

"Who are you?" Luc asked loudly, his sword tight in his fist.

"No one," a croaky voice muttered. "Go away."

"We're here to help," Macey said soothingly, realising that this person was actually alive, unless the Mahoun was able to make the dead speak. To be honest, she didn't put it past him.

"I'm no one. I don't exist. I can't be helped."

There was movement in the cell and slowly, a head peeked up from beneath a pile of straw. No wonder they hadn't seen the man before. He was old, really old, with almost no hair left and deep wrinkles covering his face. Hopefully, he'd been old before he came here and hadn't spent as long in the dungeons as Talon had.

"Who are you?" Luc repeated, a little softer this time. "What's your name?"

"I don't have a name. I'm no one."

Macey looked at Luc, feeling helpless. What were they supposed to do with this man?

"That's fine," she finally said, slowly approaching the cell. "We don't need to know your name. We can help you get away from this place though. Would you like that?"

The man shook his head in what looked like a painful gesture. "No. I'm no one. I belong here. I deserve to be here."

"Why do you deserve it?" Luc asked, frowning.

"I unleashed some terrible evil upon the world," the man whispered. "I gave up my name as penance and let the evil take me as his prisoner. It's not enough. I must stay here. I must suffer more."

Macey's eyes widened as she realised what he might be talking about.

"What evil did you unleash?" she asked quietly. "Was it the Mahoun?"

"He doesn't have a name, just like me. People call him things, but he's nameless. He only exists in your mind and that's what gives him power. He lives in all of our minds, until one of us is strong enough to repel him."

"Wait, he's not real?" Macey was confused.

"I didn't say that," the man said with a cough. "Just because he doesn't have a physical form doesn't mean he's not real. He's a parasite, clinging to all who fear, all who have ever had dark thoughts."

"Well, that would be the entire population," Luc muttered, then raised his voice. "How do we defeat him?"

The man suddenly laughed. "*You* can't. I created him, I'm the only one who can. But then, I can't."

Macey put her hands on her hips, starting to get annoyed. "You just said you can. What's stopping you? Why are you here, hiding, while he's unleashing his evil upon the world?"

The man hid his face with his hands. "I'm too weak. I need more power than I have, more power than I ever had before. Creating him was easy. Killing him is more than I can do."

"What if someone was to give you the power you need?" Macey asked slowly. "Would you be able to do it then?"

"Nobody has that power," the man laughed, madness shining in his eyes. "I can only take power from one person, and that person would need to carry several weapons inside of him. The evil entity is too strong to be defeated by only one magic, or even two. It would take a lot of different kinds of power to banish him."

"Wait, you said banish," Luc suddenly said. "Does that mean you can't kill him?"

The man shook his head. "Evil cannot be killed, it will always exist. What can be done is to stop it from acting on its own accord. It will still be able to influence people, but not have its own mind and power."

"I guess that's as good as it can get," Macey decided with a shrug. "As long as he can no longer put his plans into practice. As long as the magic of this world can be free again."

"But I don't have the power," the prisoner reminded them. "I'm weak."

"Don't you worry about that," Macey said and went to his cell door. She wasn't surprised when it opened at her touch. The man was here by his own free will. His cell didn't need to be locked.

"Are you sure about this?" Luc asked. "This could be a trap."

Macey had already considered that. "It's the best chance we have. Alternatively, we can roam the castle, look for the Mahoun, then be deceived by him again and again. Who knows if our allies are still alive. Let's try this, it might be the only way to defeat him."

Luc stepped in front of her, crouching until he could look straight into the prisoner's eyes.

"Why isn't the Mahoun stopping us?" he asked. "Why are you still alive if you can banish him?"

The man didn't avert his eyes. A good sign, Macey thought. He wasn't lying.

"He doesn't know. He's too confident, he doesn't think he can be defeated. I don't matter to him, so he ignores me. I'm not sure he even knows I'm still here. I am no one. I don't exist."

Luc nodded, as if he was satisfied with that answer, but then gripped the man's shoulders, lifting him from his pile of straw.

"If you deceive us, if you harm Macey in any way, I'm going to make you suffer for it."

The prisoner whimpered, but didn't struggle.

"It's impossible," he whispered. "There's not enough magic."

Macey sighed. "I'm one of the Seven Wardens. I carry the magic of all seven elements within me. Trust me, I have enough power for you to use."

His eyes widened. "That's impossible. Seven elements... how are you still alive?"

She shrugged. "No idea, but that's irrelevant now. How do I give you my power?"

Slowly, his expression began to change, his despair giving way to a cautious hopefulness.

"I can siphon it from you," he explained. "It's part of my gift... or my curse, if you will. I will have to take a lot though. I can't promise you will have enough. If you don't... this could kill you."

"No way," Luc protested. "We're done here."

He got up and left the cell, probably expecting Macey to follow, but she was already sitting down next to the prisoner, ignoring the wetness of mouldy straw beneath her.

"Take it," she said, closing her eyes. "Take as much as you need. Banish the Mahoun."

"No," Luc shouted, lifting his sword, but Macey flung some wind magic at the door and closed it, turning the lock. Now she was trapped.

The daimon gripped the bars, his knuckles whitening. "Don't do this, Macey! Please, don't do it."

"I have to," she whispered, her confidence leaving far too quickly. "Do it," she told the prisoner. "Do it now."

He put a hand on her arm. His skin was callused and clammy, but as soon as he touched her, everything went black and she was ripped away from her body, screaming as unbelievable pain flashed through her mind.

SUDDENLY, the pain stopped. It had been going on for years, decades, far longer than she could imagine. She'd been tortured, flayed alive, burned, any torture that could be named and more. She'd been nothing but pain, and yet here she was, sitting on a chair, unharmed. There were two chairs in the small white room she was in, and a low table in between them.

A man sat opposite her, smiling. He seemed familiar, but she couldn't place where she'd seen him before.

"You've done well," he said, and suddenly she

recognised him. No one. The man from the cell. It was him, but he looked at least forty years younger. Thick brown hair was curling down to his shoulders and a well manicured beard graced his cheeks. There were no wrinkles on his smooth skin and his eyes had none of the crazed and pained look she remembered.

"What happened?" she asked, confusion making her uneasy.

"I took your magic," he explained as if that was the most natural thing in the world. "I expelled the Mahoun from the minds of the world. He's gone now."

"What? How? That was too quick, too easy," she muttered.

"Believe me, it wasn't," the man sighed. "It took two days. You're barely alive. Even now, your Wardens are having to share their energy with you so that your heart doesn't stop beating. It's not clear if you'll survive, Macey. So no, it wasn't easy, nor quick."

"But..." she stuttered. "It was only moments ago. I..."

Then she remembered the pain. It had lasted for so long and no time at all. It had ripped through her body, separating it from her mind. It was a strange feeling to be free of pain after so much time, but it also felt as if there was something missing.

"What happens now?" she asked. "Where are we?"

"My mind," he explained. "A pocket of my mind where you're safe. While I defeated the evil entity, I wasn't able to protect you, but now that he's gone, I can at least shelter you from the pain you're still experiencing."

Macey rubbed her forehead, unsure of what to think about it all.

"So he's really gone? Forever?"

He nodded. "Until another fool summons him. Evil is never quite gone from the world. It's always lurking in the shadows, ready to jump on the unwary and foolish, but yes, for now, it's no longer existing as a being." He sighed. "And now, it's time for me to pay for my sins. I'm sorry for all the world has suffered because of me. I hope my final act will make up for some of it."

He got up from his chair and walked around the table. Without warning, he took Macey's hands in his, squeezing hard.

"Don't remember me," he said as the first trickles of energy began to flow into Macey. When she realised what he was doing, she opened her mouth to speak, to ask him what they were supposed to do about the Mahoun's siblings that were still loose in the world, but it was too late. The trickle turned into a waterfall that swept her under until everything went dark once more.

SEVENTEEN

Her eyes fluttered as she tried to open them, the ache almost too much to bear. Her whole body felt weakened, like she'd never be able to move again no matter what she did. Macey groaned and tried to move on to her side only to be stopped by two firm hands on her shoulders pushing her back.

"Not yet," a soothing voice said.

Whose though? She couldn't work it out through the haze in her mind. It was almost as if she'd gone out the night before and emptied the bar of booze. That couldn't be right though, she hadn't drunk in years. Not since she'd come back to find her brothers...

She choked at the memory.

"Quick! Bring a bowl!" the voice yelled.

She wasn't sure what was happening around her

but strong soothing hands touched her. She felt safe even with the confusion crashing through her.

Dry heaving left her mouth and throat sore but she didn't have time to care about that. There were other things making their way to the front of her mind and trying to break forth.

Warmth flooded through her as someone new touched her. She didn't care who it was at this point, so long as it was someone offering her help.

She leaned back, her eyes now cracked open. Flint held her steady, her other men just behind him, worried looks in all their eyes. And Luc. He was stood at the end of the bed, an odd expression on his face. His stance relaxed in front of her as he took in that she was indeed breathing and awake.

"What happened?" she croaked.

"We were hoping you can tell us that." Flint pushed a spare strand of hair behind her ear.

"Here." Jared passed her a cup of water complete with straw.

"Thanks," she croaked.

The water was a boon she hadn't anticipated and the sweet taste of it on her tongue did wonders for perking her back up again. All she needed now was a chance to brush her teeth and she'd feel much better.

"I was in the castle with Luc and then there was..." She frowned, trying to recall what had happened but coming up blank. It was like the memory was there but it was too hazy to pull anything out of. "Then I woke up here," she finished instead.

A conflicted look flitted over the daimon's features but she didn't ask. For some reason it felt like the less she knew, the better.

The men exchanged glances but she didn't have the energy to ask them questions about it. Instead, she closed her eyes and drifted back to sleep. Flashes flew through her mind as she tried to make sense of events but it didn't help.

Strength had returned to her, or at least it had a little. Enough to be able to shower and brush her teeth after she'd woken up. According to Flint, it had been another three days, though it didn't feel like it to Macey.

SUCKING IN A DEEP BREATH, she stepped out of the bathroom and slunk back over to the bed, conscious of five sets of eyes on her.

"I need answers," she announced, sitting down on the bed and crossing her legs. She'd had time to think in the shower and had come up with the most burning mysteries.

"We still don't know what happened," Jared

replied.

"I know. I have other questions."

He nodded and waited for her to speak.

"Izban?" she started. His well being was the top of her list for questions she needed answering.

"He's fine," Luc answered before the rest of them could. "He's been fine the entire time. The Mahoun never actually got hold of him."

"Oh."

"He was just feeding on your fear that you'd sent him to his death," he added.

She nodded, remembering who the Mahoun was but not how she'd learned the information. "He isn't mad at me, is he?"

"No more than usual," Cam muttered dryly.

Macey cracked a smile. She shouldn't have expected any less from the mage. They didn't see eye to eye even if they were on the same side and there wasn't anything anyone could actually do about it.

"So everyone is safe?"

"We had a couple of casualties but everyone else is, yes."

She nodded, though that didn't rid her of the guilt even a couple of deaths caused her. She knew she wouldn't be able to shake them from her mind easily. In reality, she'd be carrying around their memories for the rest of her life. But that was how it should be. Leading an army shouldn't be easy, there was so much more to it than just standing at the front and barking orders. She'd known that going in and wouldn't change it for the world. She owed as much to the people supporting her.

"Do you have any other questions?" Cam asked softly.

"Yes." Her voice cracked, but she ignored it. They had important things to discuss. "Where did you go?" she asked Luc, meeting his gaze.

Surprisingly, he looked straight at her with an honest glint in his eyes. "I didn't know if the Mahoun could sense me. I went to go find out so I could let you know and we would plan accordingly. But you came to the castle before I could do that."

"But the fight..."

"I'm not sure, I assume it was some kind of magic to sense danger? It's not anything I've ever come across before. Nor do I have any desire to encounter it again. Once is quite enough for me."

She gave him a weak smile. She had to admit it was enough for her too. Though she also knew their fight to save the world wasn't even nearly done. They still had a tough fight ahead.

"What will you do now?" Her voice shook a little at the end but not from the same kind of fear as before.

"That depends."

"On?"

"Whether you still need a guide or not." This time the quiver was in his voice. She wondered what it meant but thought it better not to dwell on it too much. That was one way to end up with an open can of worms. One she didn't think she was quite ready to open yet.

"I'd have thought you were the one to decide that."

"No," he replied, a forlorn look crossing his features. It was so at odds with how he normally looked, she almost asked him what the matter was. "It's up to you, Macey. Your need of a guide is what brought me to you. If you don't need one anymore then the lack of need will send me away."

Conflicting emotions warred to life within her. As infuriating as the daimon was, it was nice to have someone other than Cam know what they should be doing. And there was still a lot to do. She'd need all the help she could get.

"Stay," she whispered. "Please?"

He nodded. "If that's what you wish, Macey."

Luc turned away from her and panic gripped her stomach. "I thought you were staying," she blurted.

"I am. But not in the room." He didn't turn back to face her as he spoke and she wasn't too sure why. "But I'll see you in the morning and we can talk then." He didn't wait for a reply and left the room quickly.

Macey frowned, unable to get a handle on how she was feeling.

"He's left us so we can be alone, Macey," Jared whispered, the seduction pouring from his voice.

She felt herself relax as the words rushed over her. She doubted he was using his powers on purpose but she didn't mind if it got her to stop thinking about her troubles and enjoy the moments.

And she'd heard it said that sex had healing properties.

"Do you want us all to stay?" Rónàn asked, speaking for the first time.

Macey nodded instantly. She didn't want to be without any of them in that moment. She'd come too close to losing them all. To losing herself. She needed the reassurance of their bodies connecting and the intimacy that would bring.

A smirk lifted the corner of Jared's mouth and excitement began to build in Macey. She looked around her men, meeting each of their gazes and seeing the love and longing lingering there for her. She knew all eyes would be on her.

"No touching, selkie." Jared growled slightly.

"Don't worry, I don't want a repeat of *that*."

"What?" Flint demanded.

"Nothing," Rónàn and Jared chorused.

Despite herself, a small giggle passed from Macey's lips.

Flint gave her a begging look but she shook her head.

"You don't want to know," Cam told him, a slight chuckle in his own voice.

Jared didn't wait for anyone else to say anything and leaned over Macey, pressing his lips against hers and taking her in a searing kiss. She fell back onto the bed, taking him with her, but only for a moment.

"I don't think so, Macey," he teased, drawing a hand down her clothed chest. "I think I want to watch."

She swallowed loudly hoping he was going to do what he promised. She didn't want to miss out on what he had in mind.

Jared shuffled away from her and rose to his feet. "Strip," he commanded.

She didn't hesitate to obey as his eyes raked over her, filling her with heat and fire unlike the one she felt when it was anger coursing through her body. She had to admit to much preferring this version of the flames.

"Good," Jared said, turning his back and grabbing one of the chairs littered around the room. He sat himself down so he was facing the bed, surveying her with greedy eyes. "Flint."

The command in his voice had tingles running up and down Macey's body. Whatever he had planned, she was ready and willing to do his bidding.

"Yes?" the wraith asked, clearly amused by the situation. Macey didn't care if he was, so long as he played along.

"Kiss her."

The words sunk in and it was all Macey could do not to whimper already. This was everything she'd ever fantasised about. Them in bed with her and Jared calling the shots. Controlling them. Demanding.

Flint obeyed instantly, caging her beneath him on the bed and lowering his lips to hers. He kissed her with unrestrained passion, teasing her completely. Macey bucked against him, pushing her naked body against his clothed one, his jeans scratching against her skin.

"More," she murmured into their kiss.

"All in good time, Macey," Jared answered from his chair. "Cam," he said firmly.

With Flint still kissing her, Macey had no idea what the other wraith would be doing but that only made the situation hotter. Not wanting to be the only one naked, her hands flew to Flint's shirt, tugging on the bottom and trying to pull it over his head.

"No, Macey, not yet," Jared chided. "You'll need to wait until I say so."

She didn't respond to him, knowing that wasn't what he wanted. This was no longer about just fun. It was a game of power. At least it was power she was willing to give him. To give them.

"Flint," Jared said. "time to move."

His weight left her body and it was all she could do not to grab fistfuls of his shirt and pull him back to her. There was something intoxicating about the idea of having him so near. All of them.

"On your hands and knees, Macey. Don't open your eyes." There was an edge to Jared's voice she'd only heard a time or two before. It sent tingles through her, winding her up tighter as she realised the control he had. Jared's incubus nature would be feeding heavily from this, she was sure of that, and it would make him all the more powerful for it. She couldn't say she minded. It was intoxicating.

Hands rested on her back, smoothing over the skin as they touched too softly. She wanted it harder. She wanted it faster. Most of all, she wanted it now.

"I've been dreaming of this moment, Macey. Of being able to see you with others. Participating is even better, but there's something about getting to watch you taken by multiple men."

His words sent thrills through her as another set of hands touched her legs.

"Rónàn."

She didn't need to hear the rest of Jared's instructions to know the selkie had moved next to her head. His hand rested on top of her hair and a soft sea breeze scent assailed her nose. This was what it meant to be with them. Water, Fire, Earth and Wind. Even if Rónàn wasn't a Warden, he was one of them.

"Where should I have them take you first, Macey?" She could tell by his tone he didn't actually want a reply.

She whimpered all the same.

"Should I have you suck Rónàn's cock? Or should I let Flint slip into you from behind? Maybe you want it up the ass first. It wouldn't surprise me. I think it's Cam's turn there." A hint of mischief snuck into his voice but it didn't lose any of the command there. She was too involved in the scene around her.

Despite not appearing in control, she knew she was. One word from her and all four of them would stop. It was a good job she didn't want that.

"I think a little pleasure first. Cam, if you would."

The men around her shuffled slightly and the hands on her back disappeared, moving to the soft skin of her thighs. Cam dragged his thumbs over her and a moan escaped her lips.

Hot breath brushed against her sensitive skin. She shivered. The urge to push back against his mouth was strong but she ignored it. That might displease Jared and the last thing she wanted was for this game to stop. She was far too into the experience to cut it short.

Cam's tongue darted out and he drew it along her.

She couldn't hold back and a loud groan escaped from her.

She didn't need to open her eyes to be able to picture the satisfied smirk on Jared's face. He was loving this.

"I think you can take Rónàn's cock now," Jared mused.

"Yes," she murmured.

"Yes?"

She opened her eyes and looked straight at him, not at all surprised to find a raised eyebrow.

"Please?" she tried.

"Very good. Rónàn?" He waved his hand in the direction of the selkie who was blissfully naked.

"It'd be a pleasure." He stroked a finger down Macey's cheek.

She opened her mouth, knowing what was coming next and relishing the thought of what was to come. Rónàn obliged and she wrapped her lips around his cock.

He tangled his hands into her hair, pulling her further on to him. She gagged slightly but then relaxed her throat, taking him deeper.

"I think that's enough, Cam." This time, she was only dimly aware of Jared's voice and words. The rest was lost to the sensations of her men touching her.

Cold air rushed over her as Cam stepped away.

She groaned in disappointment, the sound only serving to vibrate her throat along Rónàn's cock.

"Flint, you know what to do," Jared instructed.

Firm hands touched her hips and she was quickly dragged back until she met Flint's cock. He slammed into her hard and fast, seeming as desperate as she was for the contact.

Macey's legs began to tremble as she tried to hold herself steady but it didn't work very well and it was only through Flint and Rónàn's strength she managed to stay on all fours.

Pleasure tightened inside her, twisting around and begging for release. She pushed it back. She wasn't ready for that yet. There was still so much more to experience.

"You look so beautiful like this, Macey," Jared whispered, much closer than he'd been before. He traced his fingers across her back, leaving discernible patterns on her skin.

Rónàn began to tremble and pulse within her mouth and she knew he'd come soon. Flint probably wasn't far behind either, not from how erratically he was now moving inside her.

She was right there with them. The urge to come was strong and as much as she tried to hold off, she knew she wouldn't be able to hold back much longer. Flint thrust into her particularly hard, hitting the spot within her that would make her explode.

Her whole body began to shake and she couldn't stop the wave of pleasure ripping through her even if she'd wanted to. Rónàn pulled out of her mouth, moaning as he did. She was dimly aware of Flint's answering noises, but couldn't focus enough on them to respond.

She crashed back down to earth quickly and found herself flipped so she was lying on her back with Jared looking down on her, lust and love filling his eyes. She knew what was about to happen and held out her arms to him. He leaned in and kissed her gently, positioning her legs around him. Slowly, he entered her, his cock causing small aftershocks of pleasure to rack through her. She was surprised she could take him straight after Flint but his incubus magic was probably to thank for that one.

She wrapped her arms around him, knowing her other men's eyes were on them too as they rocked and moaned together. It didn't take long for the two of them to explode in each other's arms. Jared knew exactly what buttons to press. They all did. She was truly blessed with them.

Coming back down to earth for the second time, she was almost too blissed out to function. Her eyes fluttered closed, sleep calling her name. She could feel strong arms tucking her into the bed and then the warm bodies getting in beside her and pulling her close to them.

In her whole life, she'd never felt as safe or as loved as with them. Even if they had horrors to face and monsters to battle, she knew they could handle it. Not only were they the Wardens but they had one another.

All she'd have to do was work out what the flames they had to do next. Somewhere in her dream addled mind, the crash of waves against the shore and the smell of salt on the breeze came to her. Not in the same way it did with Rónàn's scent either. This was different. She had to go to the sea again. For what purpose, she wasn't too sure. Hopefully not another underwater city.

So long as she had her men with her, all would work out well. They were a team for a reason and she'd spend the rest of her life proving it over and over again.

If they survived that long...

What's happening?
Find out in the next book in the Seven Wardens series, Above the Waves: books2read.com/abovethewaves.
Or get books 5-7 in a handy box set.

And if you want to find out more about Amber and Izban's story and how they met, then take a look at Through the Storms: books2read.com/throughthestorms

GLOSSARY

Adlet - Inuit descendent of a dog & human
Almas - Mongolian humanoid creature
Angakok - Inuit priest/shaman
Aos Sìth - Fairy Folk
Atliarusek - Inuit gnome sized man
Baobhan Sìth - Incubus
Beithir - Venomous Reptile, a cross between a snake and a dragon
Caladrius - a snow white bird that lives in the house of a King and can heal illness and injury
Cat Sìth - Cat Shifters
Ceasg - A mermaid with a salmon tail who can grant wishes
Cù Sìth - Dog Shifters
Daimon - Guiding Spirit (Greek)
Fàth-Fiata - Magic Fog/Mist

Fedelm - Irish Celtic Prophet

Gashadokuro - Giant Japanese skeletons that bite off heads and drink blood

Kabouter - Flemish Gnomes

Kelpie - Mythical water horse

Kludde - Flemish Shapeshifter and Trickster

Lampad - Nymphs of the Underworld who bear torches. Their light can send travelers mad

Loch - Scottish word for lake

Luch - Gaelic word for mouse

Maniilaq - Inuit 19th Century prophet

Merry Dancer - Descended from fallen angels, they now make up the northern lights

Mongolian Death Worm - underground worm

Seachd-sìona - Seven Elements

Meer - Flemish for Lake

Na Fir Gorma - Storm Kelpies/Blue Men of Minch

Seelie - Light fae folk

Selkie - Man or woman who can clothe themselves in seal skin

Sìth - Faerie/Fae

Staran - Gaelic for path

Tornak - Inuit Guardian Soul

Unseelie - Dark fae folk

Watershee - A fairy like being who often acts like a siren

ABOUT LAURA GREENWOOD

Laura is a USA Today Bestselling Author of paranormal, fantasy, and urban fantasy romance (though she can occasionally be found writing contemporary romance). When she's not writing, she drinks a lot of tea, tries to resist French macarons, and works towards a diploma in Egyptology. She lives in the UK, where most of her books are set.

Follow the Author

- Website: www.authorlauragreenwood.co.uk
- Mailing List: www.authorlauragreenwood.co.uk/p/mailing-list-sign-up.html
- Facebook Group: http://facebook.com/groups/theparanormalcouncil
- Facebook Page: http://facebook.com/authorlauragreenwood
- Bookbub: www.bookbub.com/authors/laura-greenwood

ABOUT SKYE MACKINNON

Skye MacKinnon is a USA Today & International Bestselling Author whose books are filled with strong heroines who don't have to choose.

She embraces her Scottishness with fantastical Scottish settings and a dash of mythology, no matter if she's writing about Celtic gods, cat shifters, or the streets of Edinburgh.

When she's not typing away at her favourite cafe, Skye loves dried mango, as much exotic tea as she can squeeze into her cupboards, and being covered in pet hair by her demon cat Sootie.

Subscribe to her newsletter:
skyemackinnon.com/newsletter

Join her Facebook group:
facebook.com/groups/skyesbookharem

facebook.com/skyemackinnonauthor

twitter.com/skye_mackinnon

instagram.com/skyemackinnonauthor

bookbub.com/authors/skye-mackinnon

goodreads.com/SkyeMacKinnon

amazon.com/author/skye_mackinnon